Walking Wounded

Jessica Casavant

Yellow Rose Books

Nederland, Texas

ISBN 1-932300-20-1

First Printing 2004

9 8 7 6 5 4 3 2 1

Cover design by Donna Pawlowski

Published by:

Yellow Rose Books
PMB 210, 8691 9th Avenue
Port Arthur, Texas 77642-8025

Find us on the World Wide Web at
http://www.regalcrest.biz

Printed in the United States of America

Acknowledgments

Day, for once again holding my hand through the editing process with good humor, and punctuation know-how. Even though I still forget where the commas should go.

The Canadian Addicts, most especially debra b., for their enthusiastic support.

Stephanie for creating and maintaining my web site and allowing me to constantly change my mind about it.

Donna for a great cover.

The team at Regal Crest for their tireless effort in making this publication possible.

Cathy for a thousand things, cumulating in her being Cathy.

Dedication

Courage doesn't always roar. Sometimes it's a quiet little voice that says I will hold you up. For everyone who gets up in the morning even when it feels like the sky is falling.

Chapter
One

SAMANTHA CRAWFORD HAD never been particularly good at following procedure—a dangerous line to walk when one was a cop, though she rarely saw it that way. Waiting was hell; after years of trying, she had yet to master the art of it. *This is probably a big mistake,* she thought as she hesitated at the top of the wooden fence. She threw a last impatient look over her shoulder, saw nothing. *To hell with the back-up.* The bastard had to pay. And if she played things right, her promotion to the detective squad was assured. Her mind made up, she threw herself over the top with a quick, jerky motion.

She felt her right ankle twist as she landed heavily on the pavement. Instant pain shot up her leg; she swallowed a scream. She stayed on her knees, head hanging, fighting down the overwhelming urge to retch. Once the first wave of nausea passed, she lifted her head to peer into the darkness, trying to see beyond the garbage bin on the left.

Beneath the bullet-proof vest, her shirt was soaked with perspiration and clung to her back. The early June heat wave had, it seemed, seeped into her pores so that simply standing was an effort. She felt the weight of it settle on her shoulders. As she slowly gathered her strength, she quickly scanned the area around her, straining to hear anything besides the rapid drumbeat of her heart and the low roar of the downtown traffic in the distance. There was nothing in the alley except blackness and the rotting smell of garbage. Had she lost him already?

She limped forward, grimacing as the pain showered needles through her leg. The deeper she went into the alley, the blacker it became. A sudden noise made her flatten herself against the brick wall of one of the buildings that crowded her from both sides. *Now what?* In the darkness, she felt curiously disoriented. Her hand reached for her holster, but before she could get to it, the unmistakable cocking of a gun made her spin around. Distracted by the pain in her ankle, she had somehow missed the recessed doorway on her left.

The thin man smiled as he pointed the gun at Sam. His teeth were unusually large, so the effect was more a leer than a grin. "Don't move. Don't you fucking move."

Close enough that she could smell his fear, Sam looked into his eyes. She saw danger there–fueled by anger or drugs or both. She had misjudged his probable reaction to her earlier phone call. Sam fought down her panic, fear making her hands clammy.

"Chris, take it easy." She spoke slowly, trying not to spook him. If only she could figure out a way to distract him, maybe she could get to her gun. Her eyes worriedly scanned the alley while keeping a watch on him. *Where the hell is the back up?*

Her eyes jumped to the doorway again when she heard what sounded like a footstep dragging against the pavement. She felt relief flow through her as she recognized the approaching figure, but her panic returned when she saw a second gun aimed directly at her, rather than at her assailant. "Why?" she asked.

"Sorry, Sam."

Chapter
Two

ALEXANDRA RYAN SHIFTED the phone to her other ear, scribbled on a yellow legal pad, and stared dubiously at the stack of files on her desk. "Yes, Mrs. Giovanni, I understand your Tony is a good boy. But it doesn't change the fact that your good boy had stolen goods in his car. Yes, I know." As she listened to the rapid-fire broken English, she wondered if she could catch the attention of any of her harried coworkers in hopes that they'd feel sorry enough for her to bring her a cup of coffee.

"Of course, Mrs. Giovanni, Tony would never do such a thing." *You probably don't know that your entire house is furnished with stolen goods,* Alex thought, as she nestled the phone between her chin and shoulder and carefully folded the page she'd written on.

"Uh-huh. Well, as I explained before, it would be rather difficult to convince anyone he didn't know the car was stolen, since the driver's-side window was broken and the engine hot-wired." Satisfied with the shape of her paper airplane, she shot it out of her doorway. It was as good as a note in a bottle.

"You will have to come up with the bail money this time, Mrs. Giovanni. It's his fifth arrest; I think we are going to keep your angel for a while. Yes, absolutely. Goodbye." Distracted, Alex didn't notice the additional click that occurred after a split second's pause, as if someone had been listening on a separate line. She hung up the phone and then dropped her head on her desk. She was too tired to move. She would surely die this very moment if she didn't get some coffee.

"Tough day?"

Lifting her head, she saw Jamie—her best friend and detective partner—standing in her doorway. The tall blonde had a paper airplane in one hand and a large Styrofoam cup in the other.

"Tough week." Her gaze locked on the steaming cup. "Tell me that's coffee." "Black." She stepped in and offered it. "Your note sounded desperate."

As Alex took a sip, Jamie grinned. "I was coming down the hall when your mercy flight hit me in the chest."

"I find that they make excellent inter-office memos." She took another sip and felt the caffeine pump into her system. "I knew there was a reason I love you."

Jamie lifted a brow. "Only *one* reason?"

Alex smiled. "Since you have saved my life, I will give you anything you ask." Her eyes absently touched the pile of folders under Jamie's arm. The one visible was stamped *For Internal Affairs*.

Seeing where her attention was, Jamie shifted and flipped the folder over, speaking quickly to mask her sudden nervousness. "I wish I was here to see you, but I had to pick up some files before heading to the courthouse." She hesitated. "Will I see you both later?"

Too tired to think about her partner's ill-disguised uneasiness, Alex quickly forgot about the folder as she rubbed her eyes and focused her attention back on what Jamie was saying. "I'm not sure, Jamie. These days Sam and I aren't really getting along. We had another fight last night."

Jamie looked at her for a beat, hesitating. To anyone watching Alex and Sam making a mess of what was left of their relationship, the solution was obvious. Unwilling to face the wrath of her friend by suggesting once again that it might be time to walk away, she shrugged, keeping her tone carefully neutral. "You guys will figure out what to do. Gotta run. Call me later."

Lost in thought, Alex absently sipped her coffee. Figuring out what to do was the easy part; following through was what was so hard. The two of them had been going through the motions for far too long; they had become experts at avoidance. If neither one of them brought it up, it meant that they were doing okay. Out of habit, she shied away from analyzing her relationship too closely. She would only get more depressed than she was already. Who said relationships were easy? No one who had lived through one, she was sure of that. As if they were somehow culpable, she glared at the files scattered on her desk.

ALEX WAS ON her way home when she overheard the call from Dispatch. As she was only a couple of blocks away from the address indicated, she made a quick U-turn and headed in that direction. Though she was clocked out and her day was done, her ingrained sense of duty compelled her to go, in case she was needed. When she got to the location, her eyes scanned the scene. An empty cruiser was pulled over to the curb. *So where is she?* She jumped out of the car, her eyes searching the small parking lot.

Only a wall of humidity and smog nearly thick enough to swim in greeted her. In frustration, she was heading toward the street when something made her turn around. When asked later, she would call it instinct, but whatever the reason, instead of continuing towards the street, she headed for the fence. Her eyes scanned the area quickly and didn't find an entry. She would have to go around.

She swore silently, knowing that she could be losing precious seconds. She ran around the building on the left, hoping that on the other side of the alley she would find an opening. For once, her luck held, and she squeezed through a space in the chain link fence on the south side of the alley. Her hand reached down to her holster, and she slowly drew her gun as she crept forward. She stopped and waited, patient and still.

It was second nature for her to take note of everything around her. She felt a familiar tightness between her shoulder blades. It had been nagging at her all day. She had learned over the years that the nag usually meant trouble. She shifted, trying to ease her sense of trepidation. In the gloom of twilight, she made out the outline of a man. Keeping her eyes on the shadowed figure, she advanced.

When something flashed in his hand, she released the safety on her gun, but before she could yell out a warning, he shifted positions...and the blood drained from her head as she recognized the blonde profile of her girlfriend. For an instant she thought, half in panic, that she would faint. In the deepening shadows, Sam's eyes caught hers, trying to tell her something. Alex tried to focus, tried to calm the sudden trembling in her hands.

As if sensing the subtle changes on Sam's face, the man turned his head and saw Alex. "Drop the fucking gun!" he yelled as he nervously danced back on the balls of his feet. Alex hesitated as she watched the gun in his shaking hand waver between the two of them. He grabbed for Sam with his free arm and shoved the muzzle of his gun against her right temple, making Sam cry out. Alex tried not to look at Sam. Could she take him down with one shot? *If I miss...* In that brief hesitation, she recognized the panic in his eyes and knew she had made a mistake. She was unprepared for the next moment. The sound of the gun going off seemed strangely muted, as if coming from a great distance, but the echo of it sliced through her as she saw Sam crumple to the ground. It didn't register that the shot had come from the opposite side. Alex stared unbelievingly at Sam for a moment. "No! No! You bastard!"

The thin man looked just as stunned by the turn of events, his eyes darting to his left. Then he turned to Alex.

In her shock, she didn't recognize his fear, or the fact that his gun was no longer pointed at her. Her mind went blank, and only by instinct was she able to lift her gun to aim. Advancing, she pulled the trigger, and continued pulling it until her clip was empty. She stood over his lifeless body gulping in air, hating for the first time in her life. The sound of a steel door closing shut went unnoticed. Heaving, her hand still gripping her gun, she moved to Sam, who lay motionless on her side, a pool of blood gathering by her head. She dropped to her knees beside her lover.

"Hold on, baby. Hold on. I'm here. 1033! 1033! Officer down! Main and Afford Street. Hurry! Christ! We need help here!" Alex screamed into the microphone clipped to her right shoulder.

A woman was sobbing in the distance. It did not register that the sounds were coming from her. Her trembling hands pressed down on the wound on Sam's head, trying to stem the flow of blood that was staining her blue shirt a dark red. There was just so much blood. And Sam's face was too white.

Her training had not prepared her for this. She knew what to do when dealing with a stranger, was trained to deal with emergencies with cool detachment, but never in all of her years as an officer could she have imagined that the blood spilled would be that of her lover. Nothing in the world could prepare anyone for that. "Oh God. Oh my God." She fought down the panic. Her throat was raw as she swallowed the scream lodged there. Her hand, slick with blood, shakily pushed the hair from Sam's pale forehead. "Hold on, honey. Hold on. It'll be okay." She heard the sirens collecting in the distance. "Please, please, don't die. Please don't die. Come on, Sam." She heard the soft gurgle from Sam's throat, felt the tremors as she went into shock. Frantically she ripped her own shirt off and, bundling it up, pressed down on the wound. "Help! I need help here!" she yelled into the dark.

"Come on, baby. Come on," she pleaded, as she worked to keep Sam alive.

Almost as if she could hear the plea, Sam's eyes opened and looked at Alex. She tried to speak, but started to cough as more blood trickled out of her mouth. The look in her eyes was puzzled, glazed with pain.

Alex swallowed another sob. "I'm here, honey. You're going to be okay. You'll be just fine."

Sam almost smiled.

Alex leaned her head back against the garbage bin and waited, holding Sam tightly in her arms. "It's going to be all right." The tears were flowing steadily now. Alex knew it was too late; part of her had already recognized death.

Chapter Three

IT TOOK SIX rings of the phone to reach a corner of her sleeping brain. By the eighth, the brunette managed to slide a hand out from under her blankets. She smacked the alarm clock first and slammed the cheery face of Kermit the Frog to the floor. It was the third dead Kermit that month.

"'Lo."

"There's been a shooting."

Stacey Nash sat up, immediately alert. Her hand reached over to switch on the bedside lamp.

"Where?"

"Chestnut Hill."

"Shit."

"One officer hit, one civilian hit. Details are pretty sketchy so far. Do you want the lead?"

Stacey did not hesitate. "Of course. Can you call Jim Allen and request that all available SIU staff be assigned to this?"

Half an hour later, she was speeding to the scene when her cell phone went off. As she grabbed for it, she swerved and barely missed ploughing into a truck that had braked in front of her. She swore silently. "Nash."

"This is Bill Shatts. I'm the legal counsel for Metro."

"Yeah, I know who you are," Stacey answered dryly. *You're a pain in the ass,* she thought, shifting the cell phone onto her shoulder as she made a turn.

"Metro wants the lead in this investigation," his voice came back statically.

She could barely make out what he was saying. "What? Speak up. You're breaking up."

"We want the lead."

Hell no. "That is out of the question. The SIU has the lead..." Before she could finish, her cell phone cut out. "Damn." She threw it onto her seat beside her. It never got any easier. An assistant district attorney, she had been assigned two years earlier to a newly formed Special Investigation Unit, the SIU. The watchdog group had been set up to investigate incidents where civilians were hurt or killed by police officers. The unit was a knee-jerk response by the mayor's office following a highly publicized police shooting of an unarmed black suspect.

And every case she handled was always the same: all she ever got was grief. It was apparent that the rank and file regarded the SIU as the enemy. She knew this clearly because once she had been one of them, until her frustration at constantly seeing the felons she arrested being released had turned her into a prosecutor. Now instead of helping her, her past as a police officer made things worse. The uniforms conveniently ignored her frequent successes as a prosecutor; she was regarded as a defector from the force.

She braked hard and stared. The scene that greeted her was utter chaos. She stepped out, fuming at her investigators who turned to greet her. "What the hell happened here? And how come this scene isn't secured? Who is the OIC? Jesus, why must I always deal with amateurs?"

Her investigators shifted under her angry glare. Tom Mather, her second in command, was the only one who smirked at the volley of words. He was used to it. She turned to him. "So, what do we have?" As she asked, her eyes took inventory of the situation. The crime scene was not yet cordoned off. Ambulances and what appeared to be every squad car in the city were blocking the south end of the alley, their flashing lights illuminating the gloom in eerie blue. Next to them, roughly twenty uniforms stood around in shock. Even her Forensic Ident team was moving through the alley gingerly, as if uncertain of their next move.

"What we have is one dead cop, one dead civilian, and one officer who may or may not have been the shooter. That is all we know so far." He shrugged. "No one's talking."

She nodded, then moved closer to the pool of blood still wet on the pavement. "Christ." Stacey frowned, the beginning of a headache playing at the edge of her forehead. The dead were her business. She lived with them, worked with them, and studied them. She dreamed of them. A decade as a cop and prosecutor had toughened her, given her a cold, clinical, and often cynical eye toward death and its many incarnations. Violence no longer shocked, but it continued to repel. Her fingers rubbed at the ache.

"So, who is the OIC?" she asked again. Tom nodded towards a heavy-set man of about forty standing to her left. He looked out of his element as he attempted to console a blond-haired officer. The younger man appeared to be in shock. She hesitated, but then with a slight toss of her hair finally approached them. "Excuse me, are you the officer in charge?" she asked quietly.

Tired eyes fixed on her questioningly. "Yeah. Detective Dave Angle, Robbery Squad."

She nodded. "I'm Stacey Nash with the district attorney's Special Investigation Unit." She watched his face close up, watched the anger flare in the eyes of the younger man beside him, and sighed. The reaction was so predictable as to be almost funny.

"Vultures," the blond muttered under his breath as he turned away.

She ignored him. "Can you tell me what happened?"

"What happened? It seems obvious to me," the detective sneered. At any another time she might have tried to cut him down to size with a well-worded rebuke, but her eyes registered the shock and distress in his and, taking a deep breath, she shrugged. "Listen, I am sorry that my being here upsets you, but that is the rule —"

"Fuck the rules! One of our officers is dead. Dead. Because she was in the wrong place at the wrong time. That's what happened. He deserved everything he got. Fuck this." He turned to go.

Her hand on his arm stopped him. "Detective, please. What did happen?" she asked gently.

He turned and looked at her for a beat. Cop eyes looked back at him, deep, dark, whiskey-colored eyes that had seen too much in one lifetime. He had been around too long not to recognize the look. He sighed. "A gun call came through about an hour ago. One of our officers was dispatched to the area. She reported seeing a man running into the alley and requested back-up. Back-up arrived too late to help. That is all we know."

Her mind quickly registered the information, filtered out the pertinent details. "Who was the downed officer?"

A look of pain creased his face at the question. "Samantha Crawford. They took her to Boston University."

She registered the name, but suddenly felt nothing as her entire frame went numb. *Sam. Oh my God.* Her vision blurred and she had to force herself to breathe in, then out. Her knees almost buckled; she was able to stay standing only through sheer will.

"Stacey?" Numbly she turned to one of her investigators. "They're getting ready to bag him. Do you want to see him first?" For a moment she stared at him as if unable to understand. He looked back at her expectantly. "Stacey?"

She nodded. She still had a job to do. Later, maybe she could allow herself to lose it.

Through the years, she had become adept at turning off all feelings and functioning only from the intellectual part of her brain. Some people called her cold. Her nickname in court was the

Ice Queen. She didn't care. It was the only way she could survive it all with her sanity intact. She took a deep breath and felt her throat close up suddenly. *Sam.* Her vision grayed. She closed her eyes quickly, blinked, then with unsteady legs crossed to the other side.

ALEX SAT IN the tiny examination room of the hospital staring blankly at the pale green walls. Her hands lay clenched in her lap. She was cold. So cold. That was the only thing her shocked mind was able to grasp. She didn't notice the overpowering smell of disinfectant or the shouting coming from the next room. Footsteps squeaked by on the well-worn linoleum floor. Her teeth started to chatter. The curtains parted, and she looked up at the broad-shouldered man who stepped in.

"Alex?" the voice rumbled from somewhere deep in his chest. "I'm Peter Lipton. I'm your counsel, assigned by the Police Association. I'm here to help in any way I can."

"What?"

"I'm a lawyer," he answered patiently. His clear gray eyes took stock. Her white T-shirt was splattered with dark stains he took to be blood. His eyes studied her white face, noted the slack mouth, and guessed she was in shock. He crouched down so that their eyes were level.

She shook her head as if to clear it. "Why do I need a lawyer?"

"You don't. But there might be some questions regarding what has happened tonight. I'm just here to help you answer them." He paused, trying to gauge how far he could push. "Can you tell me what did happen out there?"

She stared at him, pupils dilated. "I...I think...I shot someone." The muted sound of his pager going off seemed unnaturally loud in the room. Alex flinched at the sound.

He smiled apologetically. "Sorry. I'll be right back."

"WE ARE THE lead agency in this investigation, but we hope that your people can help us recreate the events of the evening."

The deputy chief was in his forties, but looked like a very old man as he glared at Stacey. "Hell! We want to find out what happened as much as you do—more, in fact. This should be our investigation, not yours." His face creased, ready for battle.

Stacey opened her mouth to argue when her cell phone went off. With a sigh, she turned away from him. "This is Nash."

"This is Peter Lipton. I am the lawyer representing Detective Alex Ryan. She's with me here at Boston University Medical Center. She may have discharged her weapon tonight."

"Can I talk to her?"

"Not at the moment. She has been diagnosed with post-traumatic stress."

Stacey frowned. *They always are.* She stepped away from the deputy chief so as not to be overheard. "I request an immediate interview. We consider Detective Ryan as our subject officer, and so far, our only witness to the shootings."

"I understand that, but for now she is unable to be interviewed."

"When, then?" Stacey queried.

"I'm not sure, Miss Nash."

"Mr. Lipton, I am trying to conduct an investigation into a double homicide. I need to speak to your client as soon as possible. She is the only one who can tell us what happened." *How the hell did Sam die?* she wanted to shout at him. *And what was Alex doing at the scene?*

"I'll see what I can do." His tone was smoothly polite.

She wanted to reach through the telephone to choke him, but fought to keep her voice calm. "Well, while you are doing that, please arrange to have all of her clothing sent to us for forensic analysis. We would also like medical consents to speak to the doctor who diagnosed her and to take blood samples."

His sigh came through the line. "I will have the clothing to your office by tomorrow, and I will take your other requests under advisement. Good night, Miss Nash."

Stacey flipped her telephone off and turned, fighting to keep the frustration and grief from her face. "You have my card if anything comes up," she said to the deputy chief. Knowing that she had reached her breaking point, she left quickly, walking to her car on unsteady legs. She had to get off the case, but knew she couldn't. What could she say to the district attorney? 'Sorry, I can't be impartial in this possible case because I was in love with the officer who died. Oh, and did I mention that we had an affair while she was still living with the subject officer?' She could well imagine what the no-nonsense man would do—fire her on the spot. *So how the hell am I supposed to handle this?* Somehow, she had to talk to Alex. Had Sam ever said anything to her? It was all such a mess. She felt the grief suddenly take hold, the pain almost doubling her over: Samantha was dead.

Chapter
Four

"THIS INTERVIEW WILL be recorded, if all parties agree to it." At that, Stacey placed the tape recorder in the middle of the large table. She tried not to look at Alex, who sat across from her looking pale but composed.

Peter Lipton patted Alex's hand, then turned to Stacey. "We want to make it clear that Detective Ryan has not been charged with anything. She is here of her own volition to answer your questions. Agreed?"

"Agreed." Stacey's hands clenched nervously under the table. Alex showed no sign of recognition, and Stacey followed her lead. She had met Alex a few times while dating her friend Darcy what seemed like a hundred years ago. That was how she had met Sam. She tried to push back the quick, overwhelming guilt, the grief.

"Detective Ryan, could you please tell us—as you remember them—the events leading up to the shooting of Police Constable Crawford and civilian Chris Billing?" she asked quietly. Alex lifted her eyes to Stacey and the DA felt the impact of the startling blue eyes looking at her directly for the first time. Something moved behind those eyes and for one moment Stacey thought she read recognition, but the eyes were quickly veiled, hiding all thoughts.

Alex cleared her throat, trying to dislodge the tight ball fixed there. She looked at Stacey, trying to read her thoughts. Dark eyes stared back patiently. "I...I was just heading home at the end of my shift..."

"What time was that?" Tom interrupted.

Stacey frowned at that. *For crying out loud, just let her get on with it*, she thought, ignoring the little voice in her head that told her that under different circumstances she would be questioning just as closely. She tried to pay attention, keeping her eyes focused on a distant point as Tom took copious notes in his small black notebook.

"I don't remember exactly, probably around 20:45. I was heading eastbound on Main Street when I heard Dispatch call for back-up. I was about five minutes away, so I responded." One hand scrubbed at her face as the night came flooding back.

Her lawyer leaned forward. "Take your time."

She glanced at him, then away. "I...I arrived at the scene and did not see Sam... I mean Officer Crawford. Her car was parked along the curb, but I didn't see anyone. I got out and headed towards the street." She felt curiously detached as she related the events. It was as if she was replaying a scene from a movie she had seen. "But then I turned and went to the fence instead."

"Why did you turn? Why didn't you go check the street? Did you hear something?"

Alex rubbed her eyes. "No. I don't know why I turned to the alley. Something made me turn. Instinct, I guess." Her teeth started to chatter. Though her eyes were fixed on the tape recorder, she was now back in the alley. She could hear the distant roar of traffic, the soft shuffling sound her boots made on the pavement. She could feel the thick heat filling her bloodstream. Hurt sliced through her and made her clench her hands until the knuckles showed white.

"There was an opening by the fence and I looked in. It was getting dark. I could barely make out someone standing there. A man." With a breaking voice, she related the events that followed.

When Alex got to the part where she heard the gunshot and saw Sam crumple, Stacey flinched. She stared past Alex's shoulder and forced herself to stay calm.

Alex was unable to go on. "That's it. I'm sorry. That's all I can tell you."

"Do you remember calling out a warning?" Tom's question had Stacey frowning again.

"Yes. I think so."

"You think so? You're not sure?"

Alex looked at him, shattered. "Everything happened so quickly..." She shrugged. "I think I did..." She looked to her lawyer, who nodded with approval.

"Okay. So you shouted a warning. Where was Officer Crawford at that time?"

"I told you—she was standing in front of the man. His arm was holding her as a shield." Her voice broke.

"Can you show me how he was holding her? Was it with his gun resting against her right temple?" He stood and placed his hand against Stacey's head. "Like this?" Stacey tried not to cringe. Alex nodded. "Could you see her gun anywhere?"

Stacey had had enough, and turned with a warning look for her assistant. He looked back at her, puzzled. She shook her head.

Peter did not miss the exchange. He filed it away to think about later.

"No. I did not see her gun." Alex shifted in her chair, the pounding in her head becoming unbearable.

"Had you ever seen the man before?"

Distracted, it took a moment for the words to register with Alex. "What? No."

"Did you actually see him discharge his weapon?"

"Jesus!" Alex angrily wiped at her eyes. She jumped up from her chair and it fell back onto the tiled floor with a loud clang. "Everything just happened so fast. I aimed my gun and before I could do anything else, I saw Sam drop to the ground. He turned to me and I...I shot him."

Her lawyer placed a hand on her arm. The gesture was a mixture of support and restraint. "Okay. I think that's enough for today," he cautioned.

Ignoring him, Tom wrote something down, then without looking up said casually, "That's a nice house that you live in." Stacey shot him an incredulous look.

Peter frowned. "What is the relevance of that statement?"

Tom scratched his jaw. He was the only one who looked calm and relaxed. He leaned back in his chair and shrugged. "Just covering all of our bases, counselor."

Peter hesitated. He studied Tom and then Stacey, trying to read their body language. Unable to discern anything and curious to see where they were heading, he relaxed his grip on Alex.

Alex took that as a sign that she should answer. Her face was set. "Yeah, it's a nice house. We got the down payment from an inheritance when Sam's grandfather passed away."

"Convenient," Tom commented.

"What? You fu—" Alex erupted, but Peter was quicker.

"Okay this is bullshit. You are on a fishing expedition and I'm putting a stop to it. We are done here." He started to pull Alex to the door.

"We have more questions," Tom objected.

Stacey stood up. "No. That's fine. For now." She smiled. "Thank you for taking the time to come see us. We might have further questions as the investigation develops."

"Check with me first if you do," Peter cautioned as he escorted a trembling Alex out.

Tom turned furiously to Stacey. "What the hell was that?"

"Excuse me?"

"You stopped the interview."

"We had everything we needed."

"What? In whose world? Tell me how you got all the information from this one interview? Crawford's wound entry is all wrong. According to Ryan, he was standing to the left of Crawford, holding her with his left arm. He turns to shoot her with his right, but the bullet comes in from the right and not the left. Something smells."

She looked at him. He was one of the best she had ever met, and she knew if she was thinking rationally she would follow his lead. She just didn't have the stomach for it this time. This wasn't just another case, another investigation she needed to make stick. And her only alternative was resigning. She hadn't looked at the pictures of the crime scene yet. Couldn't. Her grief began to overwhelm her.

"Internal Affairs wants to be part of this investigation," Tom continued. "As soon as we are done, they want to see the files. We can't afford to miss anything."

Stacey frowned. "I don't give a damn about what they want."

"You saw their report. Crawford was..."

"I know what the report says!" Stacey shouted. The contents of that report had slammed into her and left her reeling. She refused to believe it was true. "Tom, there are times when you push for answers, and there are times when you have to let it go. Alex Ryan saw her partner die in front of her eyes. Under the circumstances, she used justifiable force, believing her life was in danger too. That will be my report." At that particular moment, Stacey hated her job and everything that went along with it, including him.

"Are you fucking kidding me?" Tom shouted.

Stacey turned and fixed calm dark eyes on him. The warning in them was clear.

"Fuck!" He shook his head. "Whatever. You're the boss."

In that instant, she knew that she had lost his respect. She turned, suddenly unbearably tired.

Chapter
Five

"MISS?" THE MAN hitched up his pants, which had sunk dangerously below his inflated stomach. "I think we're all done here, but you may want to have another look see." He gave her what he thought was his best smile. It emphasized his double chin and focused attention on his yellowing teeth.

Alex, who had barely heard him, nodded him away absently. She didn't want to be there, standing in the middle of her empty living room prodded by ghosts. But it was no longer enough to shroud the furniture in dust covers, lock the door, and walk away. She had to empty the house, and by emptying it, purge herself of some of the nightmares.

"Alex?"

Alex flinched. By reflex, she reached for a gun that was no longer there. Her hand flexed. That gesture told her everything. Alex forced a smile onto her face, but it stopped short of her eyes. She turned to look at her sister. "Hi there."

Her sister's identical blue eyes looked at her with concern. "I thought I had convinced you to wait." When Alex didn't respond, she continued. "Honey, are you sure this is what you want? You haven't given yourself much time to think about it."

Alex's face was carefully expressionless. Want had nothing to do with it. "I can't live here anymore, Ashley."

The house had started to haunt her. Every corner she turned, she saw Samantha; every room she entered, she heard her voice. She had taken to sleeping on the sofa and waking up drenched in sweat, trembling at the shadows, on the edge of madness. No, she couldn't live there anymore. Every day, the urge to burn the house down just got stronger.

"I need a fresh start. Somewhere away." Submitting her resignation had been the first step—perhaps the hardest. Her staff sergeant had argued, refusing to accept the resignation and putting Alex on extended leave. It didn't matter what they called it; she was just as gone. He couldn't understand that despite being cleared of any wrongdoing by the Special Investigation Unit, she still felt responsible. It had been her fault. She wasn't a cop anymore, couldn't be a cop anymore. Whatever part of her that had needed to serve and protect had died in that alley, three months earlier. All because she had hesitated, an unforgivable mistake when you are pointing your gun at someone who wants you dead. But she hadn't been the one to die; the bastard had killed Samantha instead. She wasn't depressed, as she'd explained to the department shrink over and over again. She was finished. She was done. She had given ten years of her life to the force. It had to be enough.

"I understand that. But quitting the force? You love being a cop." Ashley wanted to tell her that time would heal all wounds, but one look into her sister's eyes had her silenced. The eyes were haunted, filled with a pain she couldn't comfort. She squeezed her arm and felt the barely contained tension under her hand. It worried her. "You could stay with Jon and me," she offered, without much hope of success.

Alex forced a smile, thinking of her nephew. "And wake up every morning to your little monster?" She shook her head. "I just need time to be by myself." Since Sam's death, she hadn't really been alone. There was always someone nearby, full of concern and advice, watching her for any sign of... What exactly *were* they watching for? She was suffocating. All she wanted was to be alone to nurse her wounds in private. "Besides, I found an apartment in Cambridge."

"An apartment?"

"Yeah, it might be fun to live there. Near the water."

The cheerfulness was faked. Ashley heard the false note but chose to ignore it. "If you need any help settling in..." Her voice trailed off as Alex nodded absently.

She had instructed the movers to take everything straight to storage. She would buy whatever she absolutely needed. She knew she was going off the deep end, but couldn't imagine keeping things that would remind her of what she had lost. The only thing she was taking with her was Samantha's badge. That would be enough of a reminder, enough of a punishment. In her lowest moments she thought about selling the house, but couldn't find the strength to do it just yet.

Alex sighed. *Damn!* She glared at nothing in particular, suddenly hating the house and all it stood for. She felt weighed down by all that needed to be done. Responsibility—it always came down to that. She sighed again as she slowly made her way upstairs. The sooner she could leave, the sooner she could get drunk.

Eyes troubled, her sister watched her go.

Chapter
Six

ALEX ELBOWED OPEN the door to the apartment and braced it with one of the boxes she carried. She slid the second box across the wooden floor with her foot before heading back down the narrow hallway toward the outside steps in the rear that served as her entrance. She glanced at the door facing hers. The eccentric old lady who had rented the place to her had said that the second apartment above the bookstore was occupied, but that the resident was out of town for a few days. She started back down the uneven stairs to get another box. *In a way, not having any furniture to move is a blessing,* she mused. She wondered how anyone would manage to move anything bigger than what she was now carrying up the narrow path and through the impossibly tight curves of the back entrance.

Back in her apartment, she looked around the empty living room. Twelve boxes and a brand new mattress—that was the extent of her belongings. Despite her gloom she knew she had lucked out with this apartment. Maybe all was not hopeless; she was still able to appreciate a good thing. She imagined the old building had been converted into shops and apartments sometime in the Thirties. With its lofty ceilings and spacious rooms, a working fireplace and slim windows, and the wide, wooden plank floor, it had retained all of its charm. It was scarcely a year since she had told Sam how much she loved Cambridge because of its nearness to the river and its shops. Who would have thought that she would actually be living there...alone.

Thinking of Samantha made her panic. She knew better than to let the thoughts linger, for guilt would inevitably follow. Over the past months she had learned that with guilt came night sweats and panic. Sweaty hands and panic weren't desirable qualities in a cop. Nor was the tendency to fly into uncontrollable rage, which was happening to her periodically. She shook her head, suddenly wishing for a drink. A door slammed shut downstairs, and the sound made her flinch. She stood waiting, heart hammering. When no further sound followed, she tuned out again. Crossing over to a box, Alex dug through the crumpled newspapers, looking for a bottle of wine. Unlike the crates in storage, her boxes were not marked, nor had they been packed using any sort of system. She finally found what she was looking for, then peered at the label. Was one supposed to care about the vintage when all one wanted was to get drunk?

MEGAN CARTWRIGHT MOVED through the storeroom and unlocked the back door that led to the inside stairway. She had to juggle her purse and her overnight bag, as well as the coat she'd stripped off on entering the store. Muttering to herself, she managed to hit the light switch in the stairway with her shoulder. She was halfway down the hall when she saw the light spilling out of the neighboring apartment. *The new tenant.* She had forgotten that she had asked Willy to take care of that while she was out of town. Shifting her grip, she walked over to the door—still braced open with a box—and peered in.

An attractive dark-haired woman stood amid several cardboard boxes, a wine bottle in one hand, frowning at the cork. Tall, lean, wearing jeans that had seen better days, she looked about thirty and unhappy. The profile was smooth, with a hint of stubbornness about the chin. Her dark hair tumbled to her shoulders in a tousled mess, as if she had been running impatient fingers through it.

Sensing she was being watched, she whipped around, blue eyes fierce. Her face was devoid of all expression, as if someone had taken a brush and carefully erased it all—except for her eyes. They were alive, and angry.

"Your door was open," Megan said apologetically. And was immediately annoyed that she'd excused herself for standing in her own hallway.

"Yeah." The voice was unfriendly. Alex looked at the stunning blonde who stood in the doorway and immediately felt annoyed. Shoulder-length thick blonde hair swung loosely when she moved. Gentle eyes regarded her with a frank yet friendly interest. From where she was standing, Alex couldn't quite tell what color her eyes were, and then she wondered why she should care.

"I'm Megan," the blonde explained when Alex continued to stare. "From across the hall. Need any help getting organized?"

"No, thanks. I'm done." Alex booted the box away with her foot and closed the door in her neighbor's face.

Megan's mouth fell open before she deliberately snapped it shut. "Well, welcome to the neighborhood," she muttered as she turned away to her own door. After initially fumbling for her keys, she unlocked her door and slammed it shut.

"Thanks a lot, Willy" she said to the empty room. She dropped her bags onto the floor, then kicked off her shoes with a bit more vehemence than normal. Her coat was thrown over the back of a chair. *What a bitch!* She snorted, still annoyed, then saw the note on the table written in Willy's unmistakable scrawl.

> Hello, my pet. Found you a great one! Used to be a defender of all we hold dear. Thought it would be nice for you to have a friend of the same age living next to you. She'll take some work, mind you. Seen those eyes? There are secrets lurking there.
> Love, Willy.

She smiled at her grandmother's note. Skimming a finger down the lease until she came to Alex's signature, Megan dashed her own name on the line next to it on both copies. Grabbing one, she strode out her door and across the hall and knocked. After a pause, the door opened. Megan thrust the lease out. "You'll need this for your records."

Alex took it. Her gaze lowered, scanned, then lifted again. "Why'd the old woman leave this with you?"

Megan's chin lifted, her eyes suddenly cool. "The old woman," she said in a deceptively mild tone, "is my grandmother. I own the building. Which makes me your landlord." She turned around and was across the hall in two strides. She could feel Alex's eyes on her back. With her hand on the knob, Megan paused. Her thick blonde hair swung out, curved, settled.

"The rent is due on the first of each month. You can slip the check under my door and save yourself a stamp, as well as any contact with other humans." She slipped inside and closed the door with a satisfied snap.

Chapter
Seven

WHEN ALEX JOGGED back to the base of the steps leading up to her apartment, she'd sweated out most of the physical consequences of the bottle of wine. One of the reasons she's chosen this location was its proximity to MIT and the path that ran along the banks of the Charles River. It was a great place to run. She'd spent a satisfying ninety minutes that morning burning away most of her morning-after headache.

Now feeling almost human, she craved a pot of black coffee. She pulled her key out of the pocket of her sweats and let herself into the hallway, hearing the music immediately. *Jazz. At least her taste in music won't irritate me,* she mused. She would have turned directly into her own rooms, but she noted the open door.

An even trade, Alex figured, and wandered over. She knew she'd been deliberately rude the night before, and because it had been deliberate she saw no reason to apologize. Still, she thought it wise to make some kind of cautious peace with the woman who owned the building. She nudged the door open a bit wider and stared. Like hers, the apartment was spacious, with high ceilings. Light filled the room from a trio of front bay windows. The creamy walls were hidden by pine bookcases overflowing with books, except for the wall on her left, which was covered with assorted black and white photos.

The sofa in the middle of the room was a soft, buttery leather, the paleness broken up by the bold, vivid colors of wool blankets thrown carelessly over the back. It should have looked crowded; it certainly should have been messy. But somehow, it was neither—it was cozy. In the midst of it all was her landlord.

She wore faded jeans and a black turtleneck. The long, blonde hair was loosely tied back into a ponytail. Though her landlord's back was to her, Alex pursed her lips and wondered what sort of mood she'd been in the evening before not to have noticed that body. She heard Megan muttering to herself as she pulled two thick volumes from one of the shelves.

Alex was leaning against the doorjamb when Megan turned. To her credit, she managed to muffle most of the squeal when she spotted her new tenant.

"Your door was open," Alex told her, replaying the previous night's scene.

"So it was." Because it wasn't in her to be rude, Megan shrugged. "I've been re-circulating some inventory this morning from up here to downstairs." She frowned. "Is there a problem? Leaky plumbing? Mice?"

"Not that I've noticed."

"Fine." Megan crossed the room and moved out of Alex's view until she shifted to stand inside the door. Megan was pouring herself a cup of what smelled gloriously like strong coffee. She set the pot back and lifted a dark blonde brow. Her unsmiling lips were full and sexily red. "Is there something you need?"

Alex nodded toward the pot. "Some of that wouldn't hurt."

So now she wants to be neighborly, Megan thought. Saying nothing, she went to the kitchen and returned with a ceramic mug. "Cream? Sugar?"

"No. Just black."

When Alex didn't venture any further into the room, Megan took the coffee to her. As she handed over the mug, their eyes met. Megan's eyes widened as she felt the impact of Alex's gaze straight to the pit of her stomach, and she took a cautious step back. Alex looked at her curiously, almost as if she could read her thoughts, and Megan felt suddenly out of breath.

Alex took the mug and took a long slow swallow. "Mmm. This is great."

Irrationally needing to put some distance between them, Megan crossed back to the table. "Isn't it, though?" she threw over her shoulder. Her tone held the slightest trace of sarcasm.

Alex heard it and frowned. She felt on the defensive and knew it was due in part to her rude behavior the evening before.

Annoyed at her uncharacteristic display of bad manners, Megan added, "It's a very precise recipe." She smiled. "It took me three years to perfect it. It all comes down to beans."

"Three years? And all this time I thought all one needed to do was grind them, add water...Voila! Coffee." Alex smiled, slight dimples appearing.

Megan shook her head in pity. "Amateur. This coffee is a precise combination of three separate roasts."

Alex looked bemused as she finished her coffee. "I guess telling you I drink instant wouldn't help my reputation." She chuckled at the look on Megan's face as she placed the mug on the table. "Well...thanks for the coffee." She turned to leave.

Megan watched her silently. At the door Alex paused, fighting an internal battle. Megan saw the hesitation, but was more puzzled by the sudden tension that appeared in the lean body.

"Megan, I'm sorry if I was rude last night. You were unexpected," Alex said without turning around. "See ya around."

Megan's eyebrows rose in reluctant amusement. A more grudging apology she was sure she hadn't heard before. *What a strange woman*, she thought, turning to her books.

Outside, Alex leaned back against the closed door and released a long breath. She didn't know where the need to apologize had come from. She slipped into her apartment, determined to stay away from her landlady.

Chapter
Eight

A COUPLE OF weeks passed as Alex settled into some semblance of a routine, a routine of doing nothing. She didn't make much of an effort to talk to anyone, and could spend days without seeing another living soul she knew. Much to her sister's frustration, she had yet to get a telephone installed. Having a telephone meant that people would call to see how she was doing, and she would have to lie. She knew that her friends were full of good intentions, but the effort of pretending was just too much work. She latched on to not having a phone as an excuse to avoid them. She couldn't very well tell people that she might be losing her mind. She didn't want to examine too closely the reasons for her avoidance or sudden aversion to being around people. Was it grief? It was hard to tell. She hadn't cried since the day Sam had died.

And now here she was: no longer a cop, living out of boxes, with very little contact with the outside world. The sole exception was that every morning she worked out, the habit too ingrained in her to let go of. Every afternoon she went for a walk along the river. She found the dark murky waters pounding at the shore strangely comforting. In the summer, locals and tourists came in droves, but the brisk fall air kept most of them away now. She didn't mind having the paths to herself except for the occasional dog walker or student. And they were her only encounters with people.

She knew she was drinking too much, sleeping too little, but at least she was surviving. Or so she told herself when the voice in her head got too loud. Except perhaps at night. Each day, Alex dreaded the loneliness of nighttime. As dusk crept in all around her, she watched the shadows dance on the wall, the silence deafening in her ears.

Lonely as she was, she found that on the few occasions she did venture out, she was lonelier in a crowd. That was when she missed Samantha the most. She wasn't even sure what she missed. Her smile? Being with someone? Try as she might, she couldn't find the will to go out and socialize. Having someone near, making small talk, was proving to be too much of an effort. It had become easier to just stay home with a bottle. A small censoring part of her knew that drinking was not an answer. But to hell with it; she allowed herself this one weakness.

Tonight was more of the same as she prowled around her apartment, unable to find peace long enough to settle in just one place. Up, down, pacing back and forth, she wondered for a moment if this was what it felt like to lose your mind. Standing by the window, bathed in moonlight, she looked up. *Full moon. How appropriate.* She felt the tightness at the base of her throat. Fear. She recognized it. Tasted it. Too many times as a cop she had felt that same tingling awareness, had felt the fear as it pumped through her blood. But then she had had her training and her gun to help her cope. Except for one night when even that had not been enough to calm her panic, as someone held a gun to her girlfriend's head.

A door slamming made her jump, and for a second she glared into the inky darkness, disoriented. Voices drew her eyes down to the street, where a car had stopped by the curb. Her landlady was home, and with a date no less.

MEGAN WAS TRYING to think of a way to end the evening without sounding too rude, but Alan was already out of the car to hold her door open.

"I'll see you to your apartment." He smiled, showing perfect, white teeth.

They must have cost a fortune, Megan thought idly. "You don't have to."

Again he smiled. "Nonsense."

Before she could think of a way to get rid of him, he was up the stairs and inside her apartment, helping her with her coat. "How about some coffee?"

Megan sighed at his request. It would be rude to say no. He was her accountant, after all. And he had managed to save her a lot of money during the past year. "I'll be right back."

"Why don't I put on some music?" he asked, walking over to her stereo.

"Fine," Megan replied helplessly as she turned to the kitchen. *One quick cup of coffee and I'll throw him out. Nicely, of course.* When she crossed back into her living room, he had his jacket off and was glancing idly through her books.

"The coffee will be ready in a minute."

He turned and looked at her. "Great. In the meantime, why don't we take advantage of the music?" He grabbed her arm and started to glide over the area rug.

Megan forced herself to relax. He did dance well, and she matched her steps to his. She smiled and let her eyes close, laughing softly when he lowered her into a stylish dip. *He's not such a bad guy*, she mused. *He looks good, he moves well. Just because he bores me silly doesn't mean...*

Suddenly he clasped her hard against him, shattering her mellow mood. Before she could say anything, his hands streaked under the hem of her dress to grab her silk-covered bottom.

"Hey!" Furious, she reared back, but even as she managed to free her mouth, he was slobbering kisses over her neck and shoulder.

"Oh, Megan, I want you!"

"I get the picture." While she squirmed, one of his hands snatched up to tug her zipper down. "But you're not going to have me. Now pull yourself together."

"You're so beautiful, so irresistible." He had her pressed against the side of a chair.

Megan felt her balance going and swore. "Well, resist, or I'll have to hurt you."

He only continued to mumble what he considered to be seductive phrases as he tumbled with her to the floor, knocking over a table and all of its contents in the process. Her favorite candles crashed to the floor.

The indignity of being sprawled under a crazed accountant bothered her more than his kisses. *Enough is enough.* Megan brought her knee up between Alan's thighs. Even as he grunted, she popped him hard in the eye. "Off!" she shouted, shoving at him. Groaning, he rolled away, curling up like a broiled shrimp. Megan scrambled to her feet. "If you don't get up right now, I'll hit you again. I mean it."

Afraid, he heaved himself to his hands and knees. "You're crazy." He checked his face for blood.

"You're right. Absolutely." She picked up his coat and threw it at him. "You're better off without me. Now get out!"

"My eye!" He probed at it and winced. He grabbed his coat, struggling for dignity. "I took you out to dinner."

"Consider it a bad investment. I'm sure you can find a way to deduct it." She yanked open the door just as Alex opened hers across the hall. "Out! And if you ever try anything like that again, I'll blacken *both* your eyes!"

"Crazy!" Alan scurried toward the door. "You're out of your mind!"

"Come back and I'll show you crazy." She pulled off a shoe and hurled it. "And you're fired!" The shoe hit the wall by the top of the stairs with a satisfying thump.

Megan stood catching her breath. The quiet sound of Alex clearing her throat made her spin back. Alex was grinning. "See something funny?"

Alex thought about it. "Yeah." Because it had been a long time since she'd been quite so amused, Alex leaned against the door-frame and continued to grin. "Interesting date?"

"Fascinating." Megan hobbled down the hall to retrieve her shoe, then hobbled back. "You still here?"

"Looks like."

Megan let out a long breath. "Want a drink?"

"Sure."

As she crossed the threshold of her apartment, she pulled off the other shoe and tossed them both aside. "White wine okay?"

"Fine." Alex glanced at the broken glass on the floor. *That must have been the crash I heard.* Between that and the shouting, she'd had a bad moment deciding whether or not to intervene. She looked over at Megan while she poured wine into glasses. Her face was flushed, her eyes still narrowed. "So, who's the jerk?"

"My former accountant." She handed Alex a glass. "He spends the evening boring me into a coma talking about long-term capital gains, then figures he can come back here and rip my clothes off."

Alex glanced at her snug black dress. She placed her tongue firmly in her cheek. "Nice clothes. Don't know why he'd waste his time with capital gains."

Megan drank again, tilted her head. "Give me a minute. I think there was supposed to be a compliment buried in there." Pouting at the disaster on her floor, she started feeling angry again. "Look at this mess! What I should have done was break his nose!" She went to the kitchen and returned with a broom.

Alex stood by the bookcase, bemused. "Have you actually read all of these books?"

Megan looked up. "Yeah, most of them." She started sweeping up the debris. "I started reading at age five and have loved books ever since. I used to spend a bundle buying first editions." She stood up, smiling. "So I bought a bookstore and saved myself a for-tune. Do you read?" she asked, glancing again at Alex who was holding a book as if it was an alien object.

"No."

She lifted a brow. "No?"

"No." Alex put the book back as if burnt and turned, shoving one hand into a pocket.

"*Can* you read?" Megan asked, amused.

Alex frowned at that. "Of course I can read. I just don't read books."

"What do you do?"

Alex was unnerved by the sudden turn in the conversation. She sure as hell didn't want to talk about herself. "You should know. I filled out your application."

Megan made a face at that. "I didn't read it." She walked across the room and disappeared into the kitchen. "So, what do you do?" she repeated upon her return.

Alex, who had hoped Megan would have forgotten the question, sighed. "I used to work for the city." There was a pause. "Garbage collection."

That startled Megan. Her eyes widened as she smiled uncertainly. There had been the faintest hint of sarcasm in the answer. "Really?"

Alex shrugged, not quite meeting her eyes. " I was a cop."

Megan continued to look at her for a beat. There was something there, under the surface. She let it go. "More wine?" As she turned, she missed Alex's look of relief.

"No. Thanks." Alex crossed over to her on impulse and with a quick gentle tug, pulled up Megan's zipper.

Megan jumped at the feel of Alex's fingers against her bare back. The touch left a burning imprint against her skin.

"Watch out for those numbers crunchers. I hear they can be pretty sneaky." Alex smiled, the expression softening the cool edges of her face and making deep dimples appear on either corner of her mouth.

Megan looked at her, fascinated by the sudden transformation on Alex's face. "You should smile more often; you have a beautiful smile," she said softly. Then regretted it when Alex's face closed up again.

Megan wanted to pursue it, wanted to try to find out more about her mysterious neighbor, but instinct told her that now was not the time. Just for the briefest of moments, she caught a glimpse of someone in terrible pain. Her hand almost reached out to touch Alex, but instead stayed firmly by her side.

Unnerved because she wanted to stay, Alex placed the glass on the table and crossed to the door. "I should go. Thanks for the wine, Megan."

"Alex?"

Alex turned reluctantly.

"Thanks for checking up on me."

"What?"

Megan smiled. "Isn't that what you were doing when you came out into the hallway?"

Something moved behind Alex's eyes. She suddenly looked embarrassed at being found out. "No."

"Okay." Megan was amused. "Well, good night then." Their eyes met, then with a faint smile, Alex was gone. Megan smiled ruefully. *Willy was right. There are a thousand secrets behind those devastating eyes.* And she had always loved a good mystery.

Chapter
Nine

ALEX SAW THE the cruiser just as she was rounding the corner. She stopped jogging. *Why can't they just leave me alone?* Every so often, someone would show up asking when she was returning to the force. At first she had been surprised that they had found her so quickly. She hadn't told anyone where she was moving to. Now she was getting tired of trying to explain why she had resigned. To her, the reasons were perfectly clear. She looked around for an escape route. Just as she was going to turn around, the driver's door opened and she recognized Andrew, one of her closest friend on the force.

"Hey!" The tall, lanky blond dressed in the dark blue uniform of the Boston Police Department hurried across to her.

She smiled. It was the first time she had seen him since the funeral. Part of her now wondered why he had not come by sooner, but everything had been such a blur then... Maybe he had tried and she had forgotten about it.

"How are you?" He had the pleasant, clean-cut good looks of a man who had never completely stopped being the high school football captain.

"I'm fine, Andrew. You?"

"Okay." He shuffled first one foot then the other, trying to think of somewhere to start. "How's it going?"

Alex had to smile at that. He looked so uncomfortable. "Again, fine."

"I miss you." He said it solemnly, then blushed. "I mean, we miss you downtown."

"Well...I...I miss you, too." She didn't want to be having this conversation without at least a coffee inside of her. "I need a coffee. How about you?"

He hesitated. "Can't. I just started. I don't have much time."

She sensed there was more. "What is it?" She frowned at him.

He shoved a hand through his short blond crew cut. "You

didn't call."

His voice carried a trace of something, a hint of accusation perhaps. She wasn't sure. He was entitled. "When?"

"Since. I thought we were friends. Friends should be there for each other. I was ready to be there for you, but you never called."

"We *are* friends. I'm sorry, I've been busy; plus, I don't have a phone yet." Alex's tone was defensive. The excuse sounded lame, even to her. She felt angry at having to explain herself. No, that wasn't quite true; she felt guilty. He was right. She should have called.

"Yeah? Busy doing what?" He clearly did not believe her. "From what I hear, the only thing you've been busy doing is cutting yourself off from the world, becoming a hermit. You gotta move on, Alex."

"Is that right? And who'd you hear that from? People talking about poor little Alex Ryan around the division?" Her voice rose on the last part as she fought to keep calm. *Who the hell are they to know how I should or shouldn't be reacting?*

Most of them still had no idea of the true nature of her relationship with Samantha. She had preferred to keep her personal life as separate as possible from her work. She felt strongly that being a lesbian was irrelevant to the job. It was just a part of who she was. She didn't care to know who was sleeping with whom, so why should they? She did not go out of her way to hide who she was; she was just too busy living her life to worry about it. Andrew did know, though, and she was resentful that he had the nerve to stand there telling her to get on with her life. If she were being honest with herself, she would agree; and that was hard to swallow. He was right. But she wasn't ready, not yet. Though she had no idea why.

"Well, thanks for dropping by to tell me what I should be doing with my life, Andrew. You should go fight crime now." She turned, dismissing him. His hand on her arm stopped her. She spun around, ready to do battle.

"Alex." His voice was quiet, his eyes sad. "I miss her, too. You are not the only one who lost someone when she died. She was my friend, too." He took a deep breath. This was not going the way he had wanted. He released her arm. He cared about Alex. Graduating together from the police academy had forged a bond he still felt. He had even been there when Alex and Samantha fell in love. Sure, he had been a little bit in love with Sam too, but he had been young enough to shrug it off and accept the inevitable. On their days off they played pool, drank too much beer, and argued about hockey.

He had been the first officer on the scene that awful night. If he closed his eyes, he could still see Sam lying in Alex's arms; he could still smell the blood. The smell had haunted his dreams on more than one occasion, the nightmares getting progressively more vivid. He refused to acknowledge that they might be the result of guilt.

"I don't think quitting the force and cutting yourself off from everyone is the answer."

"Yeah? What is the answer then, Andy? Huh? Come back to work? I can't even think of holding a gun without getting the shakes. You want me on the street with you? Would you feel safe with me there? I killed one officer already, want me to go back out and see what else can happen?" Her voice broke as she turned away.

"For fuck's sake, you didn't kill her! That lowlife did!" He was almost shouting.

Her eyes were wet. "I didn't do what I was trained to do. It's the same thing as shooting her myself."

He shook his head frustrated. "Anyone in your position would have done the same thing."

"Is that right?" She came to stand close to him, her eyes almost level with his. "What about you? Would you have had enough confidence in yourself? To take that shot without being afraid that it might miss him and hit her instead?" She saw him hesitate. She stepped back, her face blank. "Well...that's the difference between you and me. I was scared of hitting her, so I didn't shoot." She stood trembling, trying not to relive that terrible night. "Then he shot her." The pain cut through her as sharply as it had the first day. Her voice was soft now. "I don't know for certain that if it was your life in my hands, I wouldn't hesitate again. That is why I resigned. I lost my nerve." She gently touched his arm. "I know you are trying to help, Andy, and I appreciate your concern, I do. But I need time to figure out who I am now."

He glanced at her, then away, turned back to her. "Did she..." He cleared his throat. "Did she say anything that night, before she..." His words trailed away.

The pain slashed through Alex briefly. "No."

His face showed a flash of relief. "Oh."

She was puzzled by that, but assumed she was reading it wrong. She stretched up and kissed his cheek. "I love you, big guy. I'll call you." She walked away and left him standing at the curb.

He watched her go. "You don't even have a fucking phone!" he called out. But she had already gone in. He stood there for a while, looking up at the store and feeling helpless, then turned back to his car, his thoughts heavy.

Megan, who had watched the curious scene unfold from her

shop window, turned away as well. She hadn't meant to intrude, but curiosity had kept her watching. She hadn't heard the conversation, but whatever it was, she sensed that it had not been a pleasant one. Deciding on impulse to walk over to her grandmother's, she stepped out. Maybe Willy would know more about her new tenant.

Her grandmother lived up the street, in the house she had first moved into as a war bride. Megan smiled as she saw the old Victorian, so reassuring in its sameness. She had spent the better part of her childhood there, nestled within the love and attention her grandparents had given her after her mother's death.

She tried the door and, as always, found it unlocked. No sense arguing about safety and the dangers of living in a big city in the Nineties; Willy simply shrugged the warnings aside. 'I have nothing of value here except my memories,' she would say simply. 'They can take everything else and it wouldn't matter.'

"Willy?" she called out, walking through the dining room to the bright and airy kitchen at the back of the house. The back door was open. She stepped out onto the porch and looked around the yard, catching a glimpse of her grandmother in the small, lopsided greenhouse. A huge, pink straw hat covered her head and she was bent, slowly digging holes for whatever she was trying to cultivate this time.

Megan's mouth curved as she crossed to her. If there was one thing Megan could tease Willy about, it was her gardening talents. She had none. She was, in fact, a menace when it came to plants. Nothing survived. Yet she always persisted. "Willy?"

The older woman did not acknowledge her presence, rather just started belting out an off-key tune. Megan entered the greenhouse and gently tapped her on the shoulder. "Willy?" Her grandmother whirled, immediately covering Megan with damp soil. Twinkling green eyes so like her own peered back at her from behind small, silver-rimmed glasses. A horrified expression crossed her face. "Oh, Meggie, I'm so sorry!" she apologized loudly.

Megan coughed out some dirt. "Why are you shouting?"

"What?" she yelled. "Oh..." With a sheepish grin, she removed her hat and took off the headphones she was wearing. "Barbra and I were singing... *Funny Girl*." She switched off the CD player Megan had given her as a Christmas gift. "Look at you, luv, playing in the mud again."

Megan blinked the dirt from her eyes. "Cute welcome."

"Well, dear, you shouldn't sneak up on an old woman, you know. Our nerves..."

Megan stared at the diminutive woman, her white hair sticking out in all directions, smudges of dirt all over the still-unlined face, and could swear, despite the solemn expression on her face, that her grandmother was laughing at her. Her eyes narrowed suspiciously. "What are you trying to kill this time?" she asked, as Willy looked down anxiously at the budding plants at her feet.

An affronted snort answered her. "*I* do not kill anything. I will have you know that it's this yard. The soil is quite inappropriate for...for..." Her voice trailed off. She couldn't think of a reason, so she changed the subject. "So, how are you?"

"I've been better," Megan answered, feeling the mud drying on her face.

A faint crease between her brows, her grandmother stared down at her buds again. "Tea time, I think." She looked up at Megan. "Go clean up; you look frightful."

Again the solemn expression appeared, and for one brief moment Megan had the sneaking suspicion that it had been no accident. But surely Willy wouldn't shovel dirt over her on purpose. *No, not my dear, sweet, murderous grandmother*, Megan thought as Willy crossed over to the house, treading on half of the flowers she had already planted. *But then again...*

As Willy disappeared into the kitchen, Megan went up to her old room, the same room she had moved into thirty years before. After her mother's death from cancer, her father—unable to cope with the two-year-old child—had asked his parents for help. They had jumped at the chance to have a child around again. She walked over to the closet where she still kept some of her old clothes. The wall on the left of the closet was covered with Disney cartoon characters. She could remember waking up from a bad dream and seeing Mickey Mouse's happy grin. As she got older, she had refused to have it replaced, even as it yellowed with age. The wallpaper had been her security blanket. She grinned at Dumbo and Mickey as she grabbed some clothes, then disappeared into the mint-green bathroom. Twenty minutes later, Megan went in search of her grandmother.

She was feeling better, her blonde hair loose on her shoulders, her face softly glowing from the scrubbing she had given it. The faded jeans still fit her five-foot ten-inch frame, emphasizing her long legs. The blue T-shirt clung to her high, firm breasts, snugger now, but all in all—not bad. At the foot of the stairs, Megan promptly tripped and fell with a loud thud onto the landing. "What the hell?"

Staring back at her unblinkingly was a pair of curious yellow eyes, and just inches away a wet nose twitched.

"Oh, I see you have met King Tut." Willy passed by with barely a glance. "Well, come on now. Tea is ready."

Megan sat up and glared at the large tabby who was now washing a paw, uninterested in her predicament. "Just keep your distance, buster..."

She stood up. *It doesn't matter how successful or how old I am,* she thought ruefully, *in this house I will always be twelve.* She entered the living room and nodded back toward the tabby. "He's new."

Busily pouring tea into her delicate china cups, Willy took a moment to answer. "King Tut? Yes, he adopted me a few weeks ago. I sense a tragedy in his past life." She handed her granddaughter a cup. Their eyes met, a hint of challenge in their identical looks. This time Willy won—Megan accepted the cup.

It didn't matter how many times she told Willy she hated tea, the little charade continued. Occasionally Megan won the battle of wills and refused the cup. She couldn't count all of the times that, unseen, she had poured the tea into one of the plants. She was even starting to suspect that the only reason the plants had survived Willy thus far was because of the tea.

"So, are you staying for dinner?"

Megan dropped unladylike onto the red velour couch. "Maybe. What's for supper?"

Willy sipped her tea. "I have a new Martha Stewart recipe I want to try."

Megan looked up, horrified. "You haven't tried it yet?" The thought was frightening. Willy was an even worse cook than gardener.

"I did so." She tilted her head. "I think..." She glanced over her glasses at her granddaughter. "So, how is your neighbor?"

Megan shrugged. "I'm not sure. Some days she seems almost nice, and then other days I could cheerfully hit her."

Willy nodded. "Mmm. Poor thing. There is great trauma there. She was a police officer once, you know."

"Yeah, I know. Why isn't she anymore?"

Willy sighed. "She left. She decided she didn't want it anymore. I had a wonderful chat with her staff sergeant. What was his name?" She thought for a moment. "Billy....Johnny..." Megan waited patiently. Willy shook her head. "It'll come to me. My mind isn't as sharp as it used to be." Her tone was mournful. Megan snorted at that. Willy raised her eyebrows, her look over her glasses almost severe. Megan grinned back. Willy's mouth twitched in response. "Where was I? Oh yes, when I called for a reference, he told me that she was one of their best. But you can tell that just by looking at her; her aura is very powerful. There is strength there. Integrity. If she ever wants to return, her badge will be there for her."

"You didn't ask why she left?" Megan's tone was exasperated.

Willy looked at her. "Sometimes you have to wait for the right time to ask. We will find out soon enough if that is so fated." She changed the subject. "Have you talked to your father lately?"

"No."

Willy sighed. Though she dearly loved her only son, his inability to understand his daughter pained her. Megan's inherited stubbornness frustrated her, too. "You know, Megan, sometimes it takes a lot of courage to be the first one to reach out."

"Willy, I have. Many times. He just can't accept who and what I am. I can sense how uncomfortable he is with my life. Last Christmas, he ignored me completely. You know that. Even though I was in the same room, he barely acknowledged my presence. He still wants me to marry into the right family and produce an heir. It is easier not to have to face all of that right now."

"Your father is a fool." Her tone was kinder than her words. "He just doesn't know how to reach out. That is probably my greatest failing. He never learned to be comfortable with feeling too much."

Megan looked at her for a beat. Had it always been that way between them? She couldn't remember her father ever hugging or kissing her. All of the displays of affection had come from her grandparents. "Do you think it has to do with him losing Mother after too short a time together?"

"I'm sure that had something to do with it." Willy stood up suddenly as the smell of something burning reached them. "I forgot about the pot roast!" She hurried into the kitchen.

Chapter
Ten

DURING THE WEEK after the Martha Stewart incident, somehow Alex and Megan developed an unspoken routine of meeting for coffee early in the morning. When Alex was done working out, she would stop in at Megan's, who now quite looked forward to that brief hour. That morning, though, Alex had not appeared, and Megan had fought off a vague feeling of disappointment as she busied herself in the back room filling out an order for the upcoming month. The ringing of the telephone startled her. Her friend Sydney's cheerful voice sounded loud.

"Hi, babe! Just checking to see if you need me to bring anything Saturday."

"Saturday?" Then she groaned. *The party!* She had almost forgotten about it.

"What?"

"Thank God you called! I almost forgot about it."

"Wow. You're forgetting something? What's happening over there? Where's your list?" she asked, amused.

Megan, well-known for her organization, made a face. "Just busy. Christmas shoppers." Then another thought crossed her mind. *Alex.* "Shit."

"Now what?"

"My new tenant. I guess I should warn her about the party. You know how loud we sometimes get."

"Sometimes? She?" Sydney's voice was interested. "Does she play on our team?"

"What?" Megan smiled ruefully. "I haven't a clue. I think so." She hoped so. There was nothing more depressing than having a crush on a straight woman.

"Well, just tell her to drop by. Usually when they're invited, people are less likely to complain."

"Syd, you are as subtle as a blow to the head. I don't get the impression she's sociable, but I guess you're right. I'll invite her."

After hanging up, she poked her head into the front room. Her assistant, Mary, a pleasant woman of forty with long graying tresses, was cheerfully explaining the wonders of fasting to an interested buyer. She glanced at Megan and winked. Megan smiled back and made her way upstairs. She knocked on Alex's door, her heart beating just a trifle faster. *I've got to start working out*, she thought, ignoring the real reason for her speeding pulse.

"Hey," Alex growled when she opened the door. It had been a bad week. After fighting with her sister about it, she had visited Sam's grave for the first time. Ashley had wanted to go with her, worried about Alex going to the cemetery by herself. Alex had roughly declined, accusing her sister of treating her like an invalid. The words they had exchanged had been heated—born out of concern on one side, and frustration on the other. She had stood there for hours, staring at the tombstone, trying to remember their life together. Everything was becoming so hazy—as if someone else had lived it. Her mood was scarcely improved upon by finding Megan—who had on occasion occupied her thoughts lately—at her door, looking stunning.

"You know, you might want to start working on your social skills a little," Megan mentioned, tongue in cheek.

Alex sighed. She was being rude again, no doubt. For once the struggle was plainly evident on her face.

Megan took pity. She smiled. "I'm giving a party Saturday."

"Okay..." Alex looked puzzled.

"It will get noisy, and I thought I would warn you," she explained carefully.

"Mmm. Thanks for the warning. I promise not to complain to my landlady. I hear she can be a bit of a shrew."

"What?" Startled, Megan looked at Alex. Alex stared back, her face blank, but Megan caught the teasing glint in her eyes. The dry humor was unexpected.

Alex was about to close the door when Megan impulsively stopped her. "You are more than welcome to drop by. Lots of drinks, lots of food."

"I'm not much for parties. Lately, socializing feels like dental surgery."

"Somehow that little tidbit doesn't surprise me," Megan replied dryly. "Nevertheless, consider yourself warned and invited." She turned on her heel and left Alex standing in the doorway, thoughtfully looking at her closed door.

BY NINE O'CLOCK on the Saturday, the party was loudly in gear. Megan hadn't been kidding about the noise. Alex tried to ignore it, tried to tune it out. It was hard to ignore the laughter and the solid beat of music pounding across the hallway. Every few minutes, she could hear the squeal of welcome as a new arrival made an appearance next door. Undecided, she stood in the middle of her dark living room and thought about going out for a walk. The appeal of walking around in zero-degree weather was minimal. Finally, primarily out of frustration at not having anything in the apartment to drink, she crossed the hall. Knocking at the door and not getting a response, she tried the handle and went in. There she hesitated. There were about thirty people gathered in the small apartment—most of them women, though a few token males were scattered about. *What do you know? Megan is gay.* She tried to ignore her quick flare of excitement at the discovery.

A tall Christmas tree stood majestically in the corner, illuminated with what appeared to be hundreds of small white icicles. The room smelled of cinnamon and pine cones and the fire crackling cheerfully in the fireplace, and she suddenly remembered it was almost Christmas. She thought of turning back before someone saw her, but before she could make her escape, a curvy redhead linked arms with her.

"I was beginning to despair that all of the beautiful women here tonight were attached, then in comes my hero." She looked at Alex appraisingly. "You're not attached, are you?" the redhead asked hopefully.

Alex glanced down at the grip she had on her arm. "Only to you, it would appear." The woman laughed, delighted. Just then, Alex saw Megan across the room, laughing at something. She looked stunning in pale gray trousers and a green silk blouse.

As if sensing her stare, Megan looked up, still smiling, and caught Alex's eyes on her; her breath stopped. "God, that woman makes me weak!"

Sydney looked at her curiously. "What?"

Megan hadn't realized that she had spoken out loud. She shrugged. "Nothing." She couldn't control her blush, though.

Sydney looked puzzled, then her eyes followed Megan's gaze and she saw Alex. Comprehension dawned on her face. "Tell," Sydney demanded. "Tell all. Don't leave out any details, however small."

Megan made a face. "There is nothing to tell. That's my new tenant."

"Wow. Lucky you. What's her name?"

"Alex Ryan."

"What does she do?"

"She's an ex-cop."

"Ex?" Sydney's eyes went wide. "Christ, was she fired from

the force for taking bribes? Dealing drugs? For doing it with her partner while on duty?"

Megan patted her shoulder. "Put your imagination on hold. She resigned a few months back. According to her sergeant, she's got a drawer full of citations, and they're keeping her gun warm for her in hopes that she'll come back."

Sydney's eyes went back to Alex, who looked bemused by the woman clinging to her. "Why did she resign?"

Megan shrugged, still annoyed at Willy for not asking that question. "That doesn't seem to be anyone's business."

"Alex Ryan. You know, that name sounds familiar." Sydney looked back at Alex.

"Do you think she needs rescuing?" Megan asked, amused.

By now the redhead was leaning her more than ample body against Alex, who didn't know quite what to do. All she had wanted was one lousy drink. She looked up with relief as Megan crossed to her.

"Well, well. You did come. I was beginning to despair that civilization held any attraction for you whatsoever."

"Oh, the attraction's there, all right."

Megan chose not to read anything into that comment, but she took pity on Alex. She glanced at Cindy. "Hey there, Cindy, Sydney's just dying to speak to you."

Cindy blushed. "Really?" She looked at Alex, who was still watching Megan with a curiously intent look. Whatever she saw there made up her mind. "See ya later, sweetie." She crossed unsteadily to where Sydney was standing, a horrified look dawning on her face.

"Thanks." Alex turned back to Megan. "She was starting to make me nervous. I was beginning to feel like I was dinner."

Megan laughed. "Would you like a drink?"

"Sure."

"Come on then." Megan took her hand. Alex thought about pulling her hand away, but Megan tightened her grip as if reading her mind. She smiled slowly. "I'm not going to let you run away just yet." She handed her a beer. "You should mingle, meet people, make nice."

Alex's mouth curved. "I don't do nice."

Their eyes held, awareness pressing down on them, and Megan fought off the urge to tell everyone to leave so she could drag Alex to bed. It wasn't like her to be so affected by someone she barely knew, but Alex had her senses humming. Still, her instincts also told her that what Alex needed right now was a friend. "So, are you ready to mingle yet?"

Alex made a face and Megan started to laugh. "Come on, I'll

introduce you. My friends won't bite. Well...unless you want them to," she added dryly.

Alex rolled her eyes at that, but allowed herself to be pulled along.

Soon after, Alex was left to fend for herself while Megan got busy with food trays and late arrivals. On and off, she found herself in the middle of several animated discussions. She didn't actively participate; she simply followed the flow, somehow involved as they threw comments and suggestive winks at her. She smiled a few times at the quips being thrown back and forth. A couple of times she even had to laugh out loud at the outrageous remarks produced by some of the women. It was at those times that Megan's eyes found her, fascinated by the change.

The next time Alex looked down at her watch, she was stunned to see it was almost two a.m. Though a few people had left earlier, the party showed little evidence of dying down. She went in search of Megan and finally found her alone in the kitchen, cleaning up.

"Hi."

Megan turned. "Hi, yourself." She smiled. "Are you enjoying yourself?"

"Yeah." Alex looked almost surprised. "Yes, I am." Megan continued to put glasses away. Alex watched her, enjoying the way she moved with easy grace.

Megan caught her looking. "What?"

Alex shook her head, smiling. "Nothing. I just wanted to say thanks. It's getting late; I should be going."

Megan hid her disappointment. She had barely had any time to talk to Alex. *So much for getting to know my new neighbor.* Every time she had made a move toward her, someone or something had stopped her. "I'll walk you to your door."

Alex shot her an amused look, but said nothing. At the door, Alex turned. "Thanks for inviting me. Your friends are nice."

Megan, aware of the interested looks they were getting from the folks in her apartment, smiled dryly. "Yeah, most of the time." She stepped out with Alex and closed the door behind her. If Alex was surprised by that, it didn't show. "Well, thanks for crossing the hallway." Alex smiled at that. Megan hesitated, then said, "Listen, maybe we can grab dinner or a drink sometime."

"Yeah. That would be nice." Their eyes met yet again, hesitation in the air. Going with impulse, Megan reached up and brushed her mouth against Alex's. Just as she was about to step back, Alex's mouth moved gently under hers and it felt like being stroked. It was the lightest, sweetest of kisses, and it went through them like an arrow. They pulled apart slowly. "Goodnight."

Megan turned to go back into her apartment. It was difficult to look in control when her legs were all wobbly. She closed the door behind her, leaned against it, and pressed a hand to her churning stomach. *Oh my God! What possessed me to do that?* Somehow that kiss had awakened all of her nerve endings, and yet it didn't explain why she was suddenly overcome with the urge to cry.

Inside her apartment, Alex walked over to the window. *What the hell happened?* she thought. One moment Megan was thanking her, the next thing she knew the earth had opened up and she had fallen through. *It was one kiss!* Alex admonished herself, and yet she was filled with a longing so intense she almost turned. Twice she had her hand on the doorknob, ready, but each time she stopped. Finally, more out of frustration than fatigue, she went to bed.

She slept little, haunted by dreams. It was a familiar dream, one that generally revisited her every few days. She was running in an alley, except this time Samantha was running behind her and yelling a warning. She tried to hear what she was saying, but couldn't. She turned, trying to make out Sam's face, but the features were soft, indistinct. *What?* Something was important. Then all she could see and smell was the blood. It coated her skin, her hands, and try as she might, the blood would not disappear. She woke up drenched, the sheets soaked. "Sam, leave me be. Stop haunting me," she whispered into the darkness.

"ALEX! ALEX! COME on, open up!"

The pounding at the door woke Megan. Disoriented, she lay in bed trying to assimilate the voice, the knocking, and her location. It felt like she had gone to bed only a few minutes before.

"Ryan. It's me!" Megan soon realized that the pounding was at her door. She slipped into her bathrobe. "Next door!" she called out, her voice coming out rusty with lack of sleep.

"Hey, Alex! Open the damn door!"

Megan sighed and opened the door.

The tall, leggy blonde looked shocked. "You're not Alex."

"No. Not today."

"Where is she?" The woman looked past Megan's shoulder suspiciously.

"Next door." Megan pointed to the door.

"Oh." The woman grinned sheepishly. Finally she seemed to take in Megan's sleep-tousled hair and robe slipping dangerously low. Her look lingered for a moment, but not long enough to be uncomfortable. "Sorry." She grinned again.

The grin was hard to resist. Megan smiled back. The blonde turned and started pounding on the other door. "Ryan!"

After a beat, the door swung open and Alex's frown softened

into a smile as she recognized the woman. "Hey, Jamie."

"Well, it's about time. Didn't you hear me calling?"

"Apparently not. I was in the shower." Alex continued drying her hair with a towel, the movement causing the white T-shirt she was wearing to stretch tautly over full breasts. She glanced across at Megan, who blushed when she was caught staring.

Her friend followed the look. "Oh. I woke your neighbor up," Jamie explained with a careless wave of a hand. "Why don't you get a lousy phone? I wouldn't have to pound at every door. Do you have any coffee?"

Alex continued to look at Megan for a few seconds as Jamie walked in. "Sorry," she mouthed. They smiled at each other, then Megan went back into her apartment and Alex followed her friend inside. She turned to Jamie, who was looking at her searchingly.

"You've lost weight, kiddo. Are you eating?" Alex shrugged. Jamie looked around the apartment. "Nice place. Plan on staying long?" she asked dryly.

Alex looked around, seeing how it might appear to someone else. The lack of furniture, the boxes still half full, the emptiness. She shrugged, suddenly embarrassed. "I haven't had time to buy anything."

"Right." Jamie walked to the kitchen and took inventory of the take-out boxes and empty wine bottles. "You do have a coffee maker though, right?"

Alex looked sheepish. "Uh, no. I usually walk to the coffee shop." She shrugged.

Jamie's eyes surveyed the scene, seeing more in the fractured emptiness than words could possibly convey. Thoughts to file away until she could take them out again and examine them and find a way to help Alex get out of her funk. She might need help for that one. She would have to call in the troops. "Okay, let's go get coffee, then."

They drove down to the coffee shop for cappuccinos then slowly made their way to the Esplanade, the snow crunching under their feet. The day was starting out bright and sunny, with just enough nip in the air to bring red to their cheeks.

"So, how are you?" Jamie finally asked after a few moments, as they found a bench to sit on.

Alex's eyes narrowed and she thought of lying, but lying to Jamie was next to impossible. She saw everything, heard the truth between the lines.

"Surviving. Some days are better than others."

"What are you doing?"

Alex sipped her coffee. "Not much. Hanging around."

"Have you talked to anyone, seen anybody?"

"Not really. I just..." Alex sighed. "I just never feel like seeing anyone that reminds me of...things. I don't know. I just exist. It's like I'm sleepwalking through life. I get up, although I don't feel like it. I go to bed, even though I know I won't sleep. I walk."

Alex rubbed her face, trying to erase the pain. "I have no sense of days going by. Everything is just a blur. I keep telling myself I have to reengage in life. You know—get a phone, start to call people; but I just don't. All I feel is overwhelming guilt and loss. Yet I can't pinpoint what kind of loss it is. I know it's about Sam, but I feel like there's more. Last night was the first time in a long while that I have felt alive."

Jamie reached out and took Alex's hand. "Why don't you call? I would come over. We wouldn't even have to talk or do anything."

Alex smiled a little, shrugged. "I've abdicated responsibility for rejoining society, I guess," she added at Jamie's frown.

Jamie shook her head. "Alex, I love you. A lot. More than I could ever say. And what I see is breaking my heart." As Alex opened her mouth to respond, Jamie lifted a hand. "Don't interrupt. There're people who really care about you, who want to be there for you. Darcy, Madison, Lauren—everyone is beside themselves trying to figure out how to help you. You are shutting them out. You have shut me out. You don't have to go through this on your own. Shit happens, you know. Life is harsh. And somehow we muddle through the best we can. You don't have to be the strong one all the time; it's okay to say you need someone. Needing someone does not mean being weak."

Alex's eyes filled with tears at the gentle tone. She brushed them away. "I know, James. Do you think I don't know that? It just seems easier dealing with only me right now. I still miss her. Yet lately, I couldn't tell you what I miss about her. Some days I'm not even sure that it's her I miss. I think I miss belonging to someone and having someone there. I hate being alone, and yet I can't seem to be able to do anything about it. I dream about her, but her face keeps changing in my dreams."

"Oh, honey, these things take time. But like it or not, life does go on. And you have to, too."

Alex looked away to the water. Wasn't that the problem? Life was going on. And some days now, Samantha barely crossed her mind. She felt guilty about that, guilty that days could now go by without the wrenching pain of memory. At other times, when Sam's face turned indistinct and blurry, the guilt was replaced with an unsettled feeling.

Jamie studied her for a long moment as she stretched her legs out. "So tell me, what happened last night that was different?"

Alex shrugged. "I went to my neighbor's party. I had fun."

"That's good. You are supposed to have fun."

Alex frowned, remembering the ending to the evening. She cleared her throat, then looked at Jamie for a moment. "She kissed me."

"Who?"

"Megan. My neighbor," she added at the look of confusion on Jamie's face.

Jamie looked surprised, then delighted. *I'll have to check that woman out a little more closely next time.* "Yeah? Good for her. Did you kiss her back?"

Alex suddenly felt foolish. It wasn't a big deal; she had somehow just needed to say it out loud. But now that she had, she felt silly for bringing it up. She made a face at her friend. "I don't know."

"You don't know?"

"It happened so quickly. She took me by surprise."

"Sometimes that's the best way." Jamie looked at her for a moment, sensing the hesitation. There was something more. "How do you feel about kissing her?"

"I don't know. I guess that's what's bothering me. I liked it after it happened, but then..."Her voice trailed off.

"Then you thought about it and didn't?"

"No. It's just..." She suddenly felt stupid.

"It's just that you think it's too soon to be enjoying someone kissing you?"

Alex smiled at Jamie, relieved that she understood. "Yeah, something like that."

"Alex, who can say how long it's supposed to take? When the time is right, it's right. You'll figure it out. Just be gentle with yourself. I say if she kisses you again, this time concentrate. You might surprise yourself." She grinned, remembering Megan. "She's gorgeous. I wouldn't feel too bad about kissing her." She laughed when Alex gave her a friendly punch.

"WE HAVE TO do something about Alex," Jamie declared a few days later. The other two women who sat at the long, polished oak bar absorbed the declaration silently. Jamie, along with her two friends Madison and Darcy, had gathered at Murphy's for their usual weekly get together. The café was not yet open for the evening, and the girls could enjoy those early hours to catch up without the worry of being interrupted. The café was only a few doors down from Alex's first house, and its close proximity had quickly made it their main meeting place over the years.

Inside, the light was a soft, diffuse blue that added a soft tint to the white flowers on the center of each table. The tables themselves were round, with deep chairs and small sofas circling them. At the glossy wooden bar, glasses sparkled. There was a comfortable spacing between the tables so you didn't feel like you were sitting with strangers.

Darcy, a six foot impressive auburn-haired beauty with a mouth like a truck driver—took a sip of wine and pondered the comment. She was the owner of the café, and as such always looked forward to those few hours of uninterrupted peace. But now, having to worry about a friend really interfered with the slow buzz she was starting to feel. That was annoying. More so because she was concerned. "Why? What's wrong with her?" she finally asked.

"She's making a mess of things."

"No doubt."

"She's drinking too much, she is hiding from everyone and everything, and won't let anyone close enough to help. She won't get a phone because that would mean having to return messages." Jamie outlined her concerns as her fingers plucked at the label on her beer bottle.

"She's still grieving, James. It hasn't even been a year yet," Madison, who had been quiet since her late arrival, finally interjected. An oncologist, she would be the first to admit that in the past she had been known to cut herself off from feeling too much when a situation with a terminal patient got too painful. The attractive brunette could therefore empathize with Alex's need for wounded solitude.

The reminder of their own loss at Sam's death was still a tender wound for them all. Madison's quiet comment made them all pause. Jamie finally sighed into the silence. "I know she is, but in the process she is cutting herself off from everyone. That's the dangerous part," Jamie added. "I saw her the other day, and what I saw scared me. She has no furniture, she's not eating, and I couldn't count all of the wine bottles piled on her counter."

The words worried the duo. Jamie was not one for exaggeration. They had all been friends forever, or it so seemed at times— some meeting in school, others joining the group through a past relationship long forgotten. Despite their different personalities, they all had a common bond forged through the years—a fierce protective love for each other. Alex was the fourth in their group; and over the past year as they each grappled with their own grief over Sam's death, they had also gone through periodic worry over Alex. Jamie's comment alarmed them, as it was meant to.

"What we need is an intervention," Jamie continued.

"She's not a drunk, for Christ sake," Darcy snorted.

"Close enough. She's in hiding, she's drinking too much, she's snarling at everybody, and she's not sleeping." Jamie suddenly grinned. "You know, now that I'm thinking about it, I think she's turning into you, Darcy."

Darcy made a face at that. "Fuck off."

Jamie smiled at her, then got serious again. "She finally got talked into attending her neighbor's party the other night, and even that had her feeling guilty about enjoying herself."

"Her neighbor?"

"Yeah. Megan something or another."

"Is she?" Darcy asked curious.

Jamie shrugged. "Yeah." She did not mention the kiss, as that was a private moment for Alex. "And she is a hottie."

"Really?"

"Ladies, can we for once in our lives stick to one subject?" an exasperated Madison asked of her two friends.

Jamie stuck out her tongue at Darcy, who in turned rolled her eyes.

There was a pause. When nothing more was added, Madison's quiet tone closed the topic. "Okay then, we intervene."

"ALEX, OPEN THE damn door." Jamie pounded on the door for the tenth time.

"Are you sure she's in?" Madison asked.

"She's in. She always follows the same routine." She pounded on the door again, raising her voice even louder. "Will you open the damn door?"

The racket finally brought Megan up from the store. She stopped in the hallway, momentarily taken aback by the sight of the three women in front of her neighbor's door. "Can I help you?" she asked uncertainly, then recognized Jamie, who turned to face her.

"Hi. Sorry. We are trying to get Alex out of her cage."

"I see."

"We're the cavalry," Madison added, tongue in cheek.

"Indeed..." Megan smiled, her tone teasing. "Well, would the Charge of the Light Brigade mind keeping it down a tad? It appears that you are scaring my customers away."

"Oops, sorry." Jamie smiled at her.

Megan smiled back as she turned to leave.

"Is that the hottie?" Darcy's whisper carried loudly across the landing. Megan turned, startled.

"Shh..." Jamie elbowed Darcy, who grinned at Megan.

Megan's mouth twitched, charmed by their antics. With a final amused look, she started down the stairs just as Jamie started to bang on the door again.

"Ryan, open the damn door. I know you are in there hiding."

"I'm not hiding, I'm ignoring you," a muffled voice replied from the other side of the door. After a pause, the door swung open. "Well...I see the circus is back in town and they've let the baboons out."

They brushed past her. "Now is that nice? When we've come all this way to harass you?" Darcy asked. She stopped in the middle of the empty room. "I like what you've done with the place." Darcy commented as she looked at the boxes left lying around.

"Very convent like," Madison added. "Nice and austere. All you need is a crucifix and a picture of the Virgin Mary."

Alex shrugged. "I've been busy."

"Of course. All that wine drinking can really interfere with a schedule," Jamie drawled as her eyes took in the two bottles on the floor.

Darcy's mouth dropped open at Jamie's audacity. *So, we're going to go on the offensive.* She shrugged, willing to play her part in the little save-a-friend moment. "I hope you are at least recycling your bottles," Darcy added.

"Stretch," Alex snarled at her friend. "Fuck off."

Darcy leaned over and kissed her on the mouth. "You're welcome. Now, what the fuck is going on with you?"

Alex knew when she was beaten; there was no shame in admitting it. Standing fast against this determined posse was no longer an option. She let them take charge, and hid on the back steps as they took over her apartment. Within hours, all of the boxes were emptied, the trash taken out, the bed made. Even the fridge was fully stocked with what Madison stated were food groups that did not contain grease as their main ingredient.

Darcy made her famous avocado and cherry tomato salad, and they sat cross-legged on the floor and ate off of paper plates while sipping from water bottles.

The banter went back and forth as they teased their way through the evening. A part of Alex was relieved that the decision had been taken out of her hands. She should have known that her determined group of friends would stand on the sidelines only so long before swinging into action. She was grateful for that very predictability. She smiled as she suddenly recognized that she had missed them, missed this—the constant teasing and imposing and barging into each other's lives. The solid dependability of intimate friendships that came to the rescue when life started to win. Maybe they were right, and it was time to rejoin the living.

DAYS LATER, HEADING home from her walk, Alex was relaxed, her stride easy. Things were starting to make sense; maybe she was getting better. Alex neared the apartment and saw the back door open.

Suddenly nervous, her step slowed. She hadn't seen Megan since the party, and felt curiously apprehensive about seeing her again. She smiled in relief when she recognized the white-haired woman who peeked out.

Willy stood in the open doorway, broom in hand, and caught Alex's arrival. "Well, hello there!" She stepped out.

Alex smiled. "Hello. Housework?"

"Yes. It's a perfect day for it, isn't it?"

"I guess," Alex answered dubiously. To her, housework was to be avoided at any time and at all costs.

Willy came out on the steps, green eyes twinkling. "Don't tell Megan," she whispered, looking furtively around. "I'm on sweeping duty at the shop, but I sneaked out the back when she wasn't looking. Tea time, you know." She pulled a small red wagon behind her, filled with a flowered teapot and delicate china cups. "You like tea?" Willy asked.

"I have nothing against it."

Willy beamed at her. "Good. Have some". She didn't pour tea from the pot, but instead took out a small silver flask from her pocket and poured the dark liquid into a cup. Alex lifted an eyebrow at that, but said nothing. She handed one to Alex, who sat down on the top steps.

Alex sniffed at it. She looked at Willy suspiciously. "Mighty strong tea."

Willy smiled blandly. "Is it? Megan hates tea, thank God. Or I would have to drink the godforsaken stuff instead of just pretending to." She didn't elaborate. "Go on. It's my own special brew."

Alex took a sip, and coughed as she felt the fire burn down her throat. "Strong stuff," she choked out, knowing that a hole was being created in the pit of her stomach.

"It's a family recipe."

"I'm surprised people survived long enough to pass it down."

"Do you know any show tunes?"

Alex, who was suddenly having a hard time focusing, shook her head.

"My favorite is *South Pacific*...I'm gonna wash that man right out of my hair..." Standing in the small driveway, Willy started to sing loudly.

Alex grinned back at her. Somehow there wasn't anything unusual about sitting on the top steps in the brisk air, drinking moonshine out of china cups and watching an old lady belt out show tunes. Her mind was strangely at peace.

Willy finished and sat down on a lower step. "Oh, I just love that song." She sipped. "So tell me, are you settling in okay?"

"I guess. Not much to settle."

"Sometimes the thing that takes the longest to settle is the heart." Willy took another sip, watching with knowing eyes as Alex pensively eyed a squirrel running across the road. She patted Alex's cheek. "Time is a wonderful gift, child. It allows the heart to find itself." She stood up. "What is your favorite musical?"

Alex, still thinking about Willy's words, took a moment to answer. She couldn't think of one. "Does the *Sound of Music* count?" It was the only musical she remembered seeing as a child.

Willy's hand patted her heart. "Oh my! That opening scene...The hills are alive..."

"They're alive all right," Megan said dryly, happening on the two of them.

"Meggie, my love, I was sweeping the driveway." Willy glanced at Alex warningly. Alex grinned at Megan, eyes a little unfocused.

Megan smiled down at Alex. "I see. And I imagine you've been helping."

"I've been suggesting show tunes," Alex replied, her words slightly slurred.

Megan looked at the teacups. "What are you ladies drinking?"

"Well, it was tea time. Alex loves tea," Willy replied importantly, quickly gathering up the evidence. She grabbed the cup out of Alex's hand and tossed the leftovers on the frozen ground.

"Tea. I see..."

Willy lifted the teapot. "Would you like some?"

Megan knew somehow that she was being had; she just couldn't put a finger on how. She shook her head. "You know I hate tea."

Alex, about to burst out laughing, swallowed it as a cough when Willy shot her a warning look.

Megan did not miss the exchange. "Maybe I should start drinking this tea. It seems to have quite an effect."

Willy grabbed the handle of her red wagon. With Alex's help in maneuvering it down, she made a getaway. "Well, I'm off. I promised the girls a mean game of bridge."

Alex, head still spinning and tongue thick, tried to focus on her. "Can you make it home all right?"

Willy looked affronted. "All the way up the street? Of course I can make it. I'm not so old... Kids these days have no respect for their elders. I suppose it's our fault..." She continued muttering to herself as she left the yard. Megan watched her go, her heart full of love.

"She's great." Alex stood up and turned to Megan. They were standing on the top landing, eyes level.

Megan got lost in Alex's eyes. She cleared her suddenly dry throat. "Yeah, she is."

Alex hesitated, unwilling to break the contact. Her empty apartment held no appeal whatsoever. "About the other night..." she tried.

Megan suddenly blushed, remembering. "Oh yeah. I'm...I don't know what..." She felt herself babbling.

Alex continued to look at her. "I was wondering if you might want to have that drink today?"

Megan, who had been trying to find a way to apologize for kissing her, stopped. She had a million things to do. Sorting out her inventory was one of them. Bills needed paying. Invoices needed filling. She did not hesitate. "Yeah, I would really like that."

Alex smiled. "How about seven or so?" Maybe by then she would be sober.

Megan nodded. "Sure."

Chapter
Eleven

"WHY DID YOU leave the police department?" They were in Megan's apartment as she finished getting ready. Her question was unexpected.

Alex, idly studying the black and white photography on the wall, froze. "I had my reasons."

Megan was puzzled. "Can't you talk about it?"

Alex glanced at her, then away. She really didn't want to talk about it. Somehow, what Megan would think of her mattered. The silence was becoming awkward and she sighed in resignation. "Someone I knew very well, another cop, died a few months ago. It hit home pretty hard. I decided I needed a break." Alex's tone was matter of fact, but her mind was racing. *Don't go there,* she thought. *Don't make me remember. Not today.* She continued looking at the photos without seeing them.

"Alex?" Megan went to stand beside her. "Let me be your friend."

"Who said I wanted you as a friend?" Alex asked with a smile to soften the words.

"You won't be able to help yourself." Megan touched a hand to her cheek. "I can be a pretty good friend. And I figure you need one."

"How do you figure that?"

"Because everyone does. Because it's hard to be alone in a room full of people, but you are."

Alex felt a little ball of tension in her stomach spread at the quiet words, at the soft touch. Megan moved something in her, no matter how hard she tried to ignore it. *How can this woman I barely know make me want to feel so much?* It was too much too soon. Alex stepped back, forcing Megan's hand to fall away. "I don't want to care about you, Megan. I'm not ready to care about..."

"Anything?" Megan finished for her. When she looked up into Alex's eyes this time, her heart broke. *"You're* not dead," she murmured.

Alex flinched. "Close enough." Alex resisted the gentleness in Megan's eyes, resisted the urge to pour out all of her fears. More than anything, she wanted to be held and told everything would be okay. Feeling Megan's closeness, she panicked; she didn't want to need again. She turned all business. She knew she was in full flight but was unable to stop herself.

"You know, maybe we can skip that drink for now. I'm sorry, I just remembered something I have to do."

Megan took her cue. "Maybe some other time, then." She watched Alex go, and once the door closed, threw a cushion against it, cursing herself for a fool. *Damn. I should have left it alone. Damn. Damn. Damn.*

Alex left, fear and panic warring inside of her. Every time she thought she had turned a corner, she lost a step. It was like she was swimming against the tide and was unable to quite reach the shore.

Megan had every right to ask, to be curious. Why shouldn't she? But, instead of behaving like a mature adult, she had fled, unwilling to talk about it. *Why? Am I scared of her questions? Or, is it the answers I am running away from?* She din't want to look too closely there. Pride. She had always had too much of it. Being the best had always been so important to her. Being right. Wasn't that part of the reason she had been unable to forgive Samantha for her affair the year before: her inability to accept that people made mistakes? And now for months she had fought the realization that she was human like everyone else. She had screwed up, and her mistake had caused the death of her girlfriend. And maybe, just maybe, she had been just as much to blame for Sam's affair. Wasn't that the eye-opener she was fleeing from?

She got in her car and started driving. 'How can anyone ever live up to those impossibly high standards?' That's what Sam had shouted the night before her death. It had been a stupid fight, one more in a long line of pointless arguments. It was as if the fighting had compensated for the fact that they had run out of things to talk about.

She suddenly stopped the car and sat there staring at the little brick bungalow with its beige trim and white windows. Unconsciously, she had driven to her house. It didn't feel like hers anymore; she felt no connection to it. The drive needed shoveling. The paint was peeling from the small front porch. It looked desolate.

Alex got out of the car and simply stared for a long moment, thinking back to the closing and remembering the excitement she had felt in its ownership. All those possibilities had ended with a single shot. Or had they ended years before when she and Sam had fallen out of love? With a heavy heart, she turned her key in the lock and went in. The stillness enveloped her; the musty smell of closed-in rooms assailed her nostrils. She went through to the living room, her footsteps echoing on the hardwood floor, then she sat down on the floor and waited for the ghosts.

SEVERAL HOURS LATER, Megan was faking interest in a book when she heard the front door crash and then heavy footsteps on the stairs. At the second crash, she bolted to the door. Alex was leaning against the wall, trying to find her keys. When she saw Megan, she straightened—not very successfully—and peered at her neighbor. "Hi!" She was drunk. Her eyes tried to focus on Megan. "I had a beer." She enunciated each word carefully.

Megan shook her head. "Just one?"

"Yep. Nope." Alex started to close her eyes, but everything started to spin. "Whoa!"

"Where are your keys?"

"Dunno. In my pocket."

"Which one?"

Alex shrugged and almost fell.

Megan sighed. She grabbed her tenant and wrapped an arm around her waist. "Come on." She dragged Alex into her apartment. They stumbled to the couch. "You didn't drive in this condition, did you?"

"Of course not. I flew." Alex collapsed onto her side and closed her eyes.

Megan eyed her clothes, but decided against trying to take any of them off. She pulled her shoes off, grabbed a blanket from the back of the couch and covered her.

Alex opened her eyes. "God! Your mouth is to die for." Her eyes closed. "But let's get this straight: I don't want to sleep with you."

"Well, that certainly puts me in my place."

"You've got complications written all over you. I just want to be alone. I think."

"I guess that kills any hopes I've been harboring. But don't worry, I'll get over it."

"They didn't come."

"Who?"

"The ghosts."

Puzzled, Megan looked at her, then had to smile. *She looks awfully cute,* she thought. *All drunk and surly and heavy-eyed.* She pulled the blanket to Alex's chin and tucked it neatly around her. "Here you go, nice and cozy." Acting on impulse, she leaned over and kissed the end of her nose. "Go to sleep, Alex. You're going to feel like hell tomorrow." She turned to leave the room.

"Megan?"

"Yes?"

"You are the most beautiful woman I have ever seen."

Megan felt the pull of attraction at the whispered words, but stopped herself from crossing back. "I'll see you in the morning." She smiled ruefully at the unmistakable sound of snoring.

THE SMELL OF coffee woke Alex. She opened her eyes, then wished she hadn't and closed them with a groan. After a pause, she chanced another look, but there was no mistaking the pounding in her head. One hand feebly reached for her forehead and pressed gingerly against it. Maybe if she held her head, it wouldn't fall off. She slowly sat up. Even her teeth were hurting. *What did I do last night?* It slowly dawned on her that she was sitting on a couch and not her bed, and that someone else was in the room. She peered painfully through her fingers.

Megan was watching her silently, then she walked over and held out her hand. "Here."

Alex tried to focus on the upturned palm. "What is it?" she croaked out, wincing at the noise.

"Aspirin."

She took the tablets and the glass of water and swallowed them together.

Megan returned with a mug of steaming black coffee. "Have some coffee. I have to go downstairs to open the store. I think it's safe to leave you alone..."

Alex looked at her and wished she hadn't. Her eyes hurt. She pressed her hands against her eyelids.

"Have a shower or whatever you need."

"I think I'm just going to crawl across the hall to look for my head."

Megan, refusing to show any pity, hid a smile.

"Megan..." Alex's voice stopped her at the door. Hand on the door handle she turned. "I...I do...Thanks," she finished helplessly.

Megan smiled as she nodded. "See you later."

Alex carefully made her way downstairs a few hours later, trying to time each of her steps to counter-synch with the pounding in her head. A shower had almost revived her. Almost. Approaching the bottom landing, she heard a loud crash, followed by a muffled curse. She paused, listening, before she entered the store. Megan was standing beside a table that had held a display of the latest bestsellers. Alex focused on her face. It was pale, with anger dancing on the edges of it. She kept her voice carefully neutral. "Is something wrong?"

"Wrong?" Megan laughed, a hint of hysteria creeping in. "No. I just got a letter from my father."

"Yeah?" Alex was perplexed. "Bad news?"

"In a matter of speaking. It's more of a summons than a letter, really." Megan handed her the thin sheet of blue paper and turned away, busying herself with the fallen books.

Alex skimmed the letter. "It sounds like an invitation to a party."

"You have to read between the lines." Impatiently, Megan pushed her hair back. "You always have to read between the lines." The color had returned to her cheeks. She focused on Alex. "How are you feeling?"

Alex shrugged a little sheepish. "Better. I'm sorry about last night."

"Well, it's not every day that a beautiful woman comes crashing through my door." Megan looked at her for a moment.

Alex was puzzling over the letter, and she missed the yearning in Megan's eyes. "So, what's wrong with this party?" Not getting a response, she looked up, and her gaze collided with Megan's. "What?"

"Come with me," Megan said impulsively.

"What? Where?" There was panic in her tone.

"To the party."

Alex was already shaking her head. "I don't...I'm not good..."

"Please."

Alex looked at her helplessly. *God, she is stunning.* Her eyes touched Megan's mouth and lingered. They stood inches apart, breath mingling, anticipation there just below the surface—when the sharp sound of the bell from the opening door crashed through. They jumped apart guiltily, Megan blushing furiously as she turned toward the new arrival.

Maybe complications wouldn't be so bad, Alex thought, hesitating for a moment. She surprised them both by giving in unexpectedly. "I'll see you Saturday night, then."

Megan's smile was slow and sexy as she nodded and turned to her customer.

"GET IN HERE! I'm a desperate woman!" Alex pulled an amused Jamie into her apartment.

Jamie glanced about with approval. Alex had furnished the room with a dark green loveseat and a plaid chair in bright reds, greens, and golds. The room still lacked the little personal touches that made a room a home, but this was definitely progress. "So, what's the emergency?'

"I have nothing to wear!"

Jamie glanced at Alex, dressed in a loose T-shirt that fell almost to her knees and nothing else, and smiled. "Apparently."

Alex dragged her into the bedroom. Her new bed was covered with a mountain of clothes. Alex waved at them. "See? Nothing." She pushed a hand through her hair and suddenly eyed Jamie. There was a dangerous light in her eyes. "That's nice. Is it new?"

Jamie shook her head. "No way." Alex advanced as Jamie retreated, laughing. "Back off, Alex, I mean it." Alex chased her back into the living room. Jamie howled as Alex lunged and they both fell on the couch.

"Take your clothes off."

Jamie laughed at that. "Has that ever worked for you?"

Alex grinned. "You should know."

Jamie waved that away. "Well, I didn't let you borrow clothes when we were in grade school, and I'm not about to let you start now."

Alex made a noise that sounded suspiciously like a snort. "That's because I had boobs and you didn't. Come on, James! I'm desperate." After a brief tug of war, she was able to pull the soft blue cashmere sweater off of her friend. "I have a date Saturday," she moaned.

Jamie relaxed back against the couch and crossed her arms over her chest. "Okay, you get my top...but nothing else," she warned at Alex's proprietary look at her cream-colored suede pants.

"Our first date. Oh my God, I'm starting to hyperventilate."

Jamie smiled and kissed her. "Take a deep breath. Auntie Jamie is here to make it all better."

"I can't remember the last time I went on a date. Am I expected to bring something?"

"Where are you going?"

"Her father's place; he's giving a party. I don't think she really wants to go." She settled down beside Jamie. "Maybe I should cancel. Damn, I don't even know if it's formal or anything." She rushed through her thoughts. "You should have seen her face just after she got the invitation. I mean, she looked angry, but at the same time—just lost. I still don't get why he just didn't call to invite her. That's weird. You know?" She caught Jamie's wide grin. "What?"

Jamie continued grinning. "You're babbling. That's so cute."

Alex frowned at that. "I am not." *Am I?* She went on. "I got drunk last night. I don't even remember getting home, and then next thing you know, I'm waking up at Megan's and she..."

"Whoa! Back up a minute." Jamie sat up. "You slept with Megan?"

"Did I say that? I said I woke up at Megan's." Looking sheep-ish, Alex shrugged. "I passed out on her couch."

"Way to make a good impression."

Alex made a face at that. "I was celebrating." Her voice was suddenly quiet. "Jamie, I went home yesterday."

Jamie was having a hard time keeping up. "I thought you passed out at Megan's."

"I did. But before that, I went back to my house."

Surprised, Jamie swung her legs around to sit beside Alex. "You did?"

"Yeah. I went in, sat down in the middle of the living room, and cried like a baby."

"Oh, honey! Why didn't you call me?"

"I didn't have a phone," they finished together.

Jamie shook her head. "What made you go?"

"I don't know. Last night Megan tried to talk to me about what happened, and I literally ran out like a coward. I just found myself driving over there. I guess I needed to go. I think I went to say goodbye. I have been avoiding moving on." Alex looked at Jamie, then looked down at her hands.

"I'm putting the house up for sale."

Jamie studied her, hiding her surprise. "That's a big step."

"Yeah. But now that I've made up my mind, it's almost a relief, you know? I don't have that decision hanging over my head. While I was sitting there, I started thinking back to those last months with Sam. I was so unhappy. I mean, deep down inside I wanted to leave. When I found out about her affair, I wasn't as upset as I should have been. My pride was hurt, but not my heart, you know? I was angrier with her for not telling me who the other woman was. As if that would have made a difference. Looking back, it's pretty obvious that she was unhappy too." She looked at Jamie, who nod-ded in agreement.

"We had been going through the motions for years. I loved her because she was my best friend and because we had a history together. In the end, neither one of us was able to finally do the deed and walk away. Emotionally, I had walked away years before, and I guess she had too. Funny how you forget stuff like that." She took a deep breath.

"Sitting in the living room, I remembered what I felt when I was packing up the stuff to move out after she died. For a split sec-ond I felt relief that she had died, so that I didn't have to be the one to say it was over."

She scrubbed at her face. "God, I'm such a shit. Maybe that is why I'm feeling so guilty. All this time I've been thinking that I didn't try hard enough to save her. You know, maybe subconsciously... " She looked at her hands.

Jamie looked at her, stunned. Her frustration with Alex finally broke through her concern. "Give me a break! That is the stupidest thing I've ever heard. You're not responsible for her death, you moron. Some lunatic high on drugs is. And as awful and as sad it is to mention it now, Sam acted recklessly that night. She did not wait for back-up."

Jamie took her hand. "You know what the problem is? You are starting to realize what the rest of us already knew: you had a human frailty. I bet you've had a hell of a time adjusting to the fact that you're not perfect. Now that you have, you'll probably be a better cop when you put that badge back on. But to say that you caused Sam's death because you wanted to leave her is just plain..." She shook her head. "I can't even think of a word strong enough to describe it. Fucked, that's it."

Alex had to smile at Jamie, she looked so upset. "Okay, I get the picture."

"Do you? I'm not so sure. I love you; we've been friends forever. But you know what, Alex? I have had it. It's almost like you're enjoying feeling sorry for yourself. I think you are taking the easy way out. You've cut yourself off from your friends. That way you don't have to deal with it, with life. Everyone tries to leave you alone because you're broken hearted, but I'm getting tired of handling you with kid gloves. Stop wallowing in this shit. You deserve better than this. It's time for you to move on."

It had been bottling up for months and now that it was out, Jamie was as stunned as Alex, fighting for calm as she rubbed a shaky hand over her face. *Well, hell.* She almost never lost her temper, but when she did, it was always an eruption that cooled just as quickly. In a softer voice, she added, "I miss you, the Alex I know; I want my best friend back. We all miss you, dammit! And besides, I'm tired of fending off Madison and Darcy."

Alex swallowed the quick retort that sprang up. Her first reaction was to be insulted, but of course, as always, Jamie was right. This time she would admit it. "You're right. Absolutely. That's why I'm selling the house."

Jamie, who had opened her mouth to produce an additional argument, closed it with a snap and frowned at Alex. *Is she just saying that?*

The knock at the door made them both jump. Alex's gaze flickered to the door.

"Alex? It's Megan..." the voice called out after a pause.

"Damn!" Alex jumped off the couch and turned to Jamie. "It's Megan!"

Jamie didn't reply, too busy looking for her sweater. She

pulled it on, almost ripping it in her haste.

Megan had turned away from the door by the time Alex opened it. "Hi."

"I'm sorry, I forgot to tell you that the party is a dressy thing." Her eyes flickered to Jamie, took stock, then returned to Alex, took in her lack of clothes, and watched the slow blush tint Alex's cheeks. She tried to ignore the quick stab of jealousy. "Is that going to be a problem?"

"No. I think I can handle it." Alex stopped herself from apologizing. She had no reason to feel so defensive. She shifted inside the door.

"Nice to see you again," Megan called out to Jamie, then without another word she went back to her apartment.

Alex turned to Jamie and her eyes widened as she took in Jamie's sweater, which was inside out, and then noticed her own lack of attire. "Well, hell..."

AFTER GIVING ALEX directions to her father's house, Megan reverted to silence. She was uneasy about the party, annoyed at herself for agreeing to the command appearance. *Why couldn't I just once ignore family obligations?* She also knew that a great deal of her frustration was directed internally at her reaction to finding Alex half naked with Jamie. Jealousy was an unfamiliar emotion for her and it threw her. She bit down on her lower lip. For the first time in a long while, she felt out of her depth with someone, unsure of her next step.

Alex studied the cool profile. *She's upset; that much is obvious.* But she couldn't think of any reason Megan should be angry with her. She hadn't done anything wrong, yet there she was feeling guilty. She hated that. Worse, she hated the look on Megan's face. Her fingers drummed impatiently on the steering wheel. Finally she pulled the car over to the curb. "Megan?" Lost in her own thoughts, Megan turned her head slowly. "Jamie has been my best friend since grade school. We're like sisters."

"You don't owe me an explanation," Megan said quietly, looking down at her hands.

"I know I don't," Alex almost snarled. "I just wanted to tell you."

"Okay."

Alex continued to look at her, frustrated by the distance between them. Acting on impulse, she surprised her passenger by pulling her close. She brought her mouth down on Megan's in a kiss tasting of frustration and an underlying hint of wild darkness that had the blood draining out of Megan's head.

Oh God, my God, was all she had a chance to think. Or perhaps she groaned it, as her lips parted helplessly under Alex's. It was quick, seconds only, but when Alex released her, Megan knew that she had lost something.

Alex continued to look at her, fighting down the urge to take more, to lose herself in that erotically charged mouth. "You are starting to matter."

Megan read the frustration that quickly flared in Alex's eyes at having to admit need. It almost delighted her, and Megan felt her own irritation dissolve. Every time she thought she understood the situation, Alex did something that turned everything on its head. She wetted her lips and watched Alex's eyes follow the movement of her tongue. *Oh my.* She had to draw in a shaky breath. She would barely last the night.

Alex drew up in front of the address Megan had given her and just stared in awe at the sculpted stone house at the end of the curving driveway. "Jesus! This is your house?" A high brick wall had hidden the house from the road. Layers of snow hid the perfectly manicured lawn and rose bushes.

"It's my *father's* house."

Alex looked at her quizzically, but said nothing more. A line of exotic cars was already parked on the south side of the driveway, so they pulled up by the four-car garage on the left.

A uniformed attendant materialized out of nowhere. "Good evening, Miss. I'll park it for you."

Alex directed a helpless look towards Megan, but her passenger was already out of the car and starting toward the large oak door. Alex shrugged and handed him the keys. She followed Megan slowly, taking stock of the imposing house, admiring the lights glowing behind tall stained glass windows.

Inside, Alex grabbed a couple of flutes of champagne from a passing waiter and handed a glass to Megan. "Why didn't you tell me your family is stinking rich?"

"Does it matter?"

Alex studied Megan's face. There was an edge below the question. "No."

Megan sipped her champagne, felt the bubbles dance on her tongue. "The subject never came up." She smiled coolly. "Besides, my father's financial standing has nothing to do with me."

Alex looked around the large ballroom. It was an imposing room, made more so by the gleaming chandeliers overhead and marble columns. A string quartet was playing Vivaldi on a small platform by the ceiling to floor window. *Mother would kill to have this,* she thought, amused. "Well, you have a beautiful home."

Megan turned to look at her. "It's a museum. It never was my home."

Alex was about to ask why when a well put together woman of fifty approached. Her blonde hair was cut in a smooth bob, the color expertly done. She smiled as she neared. "Hello, Megan." They exchanged air kisses. "Glad you could make it; who is your friend?"

Megan turned to make the introductions. "This is Alex. Alex, my stepmother, Eileen."

The woman smiled again. "Nice to meet you, Alex." She turned to Megan, effectively dismissing Alex. "Your father is talking to the mayor, but I know he will be thrilled you came."

Megan smiled, playing along. "Of course. I wouldn't have missed it for the world."

Eileen smiled back, then her eyes caught new arrivals. "Bart! Donna!" she called out. "So glad you could come." She smiled a perfect hostess smile as she took her leave. "Excuse me."

Alex watched her go, amused beyond words.

Megan watched her stepmother's simpering departure, certain now that it had been a mistake to come. She turned to Alex. "I don't know about you, but I need something stronger than bubbles." She lifted her empty glass. "Want something else?"

Alex smiled. "Sure." She watched Megan make her way through the crowd to a bar that had been set up on the other side of the room. The desire for her was there, just below the surface.

"Hello there!" At the words, Alex turned, and had to grin at the sight that greeted her. Willy was eye-catching in a flowered dress of bright yellows and blues. A large string of pearls rested on her ample bosom.

"Very 'Royal Family'."

Willy beamed. "Thank you. I thought so too." Unconsciously, Alex turned her head to look for Megan. Willy smiled, her eyes knowing. "She is lovely, isn't she?"

Alex turned to her, embarrassed at being so transparent. Is *it that obvious?*

"Her heart is kind, but it bruises easily. Just like yours, I imagine," Willy added.

Alex's eyes narrowed suspiciously. "You're not trying to play matchmaker, are you?"

Willy's green eyes twinkled. "No need. Fate has it well in hand." Before Alex could respond to that, Willy interjected, "David, darling, how dashing you look!"

A distinguished man in his mid-fifties approached. The high cheekbones and strong chin hinted of Megan. He bent down from his considerable height and kissed Willy. In his eyes, Alex read a mixture of exasperation and genuine affection. "You look charming, Mother." His hazel colored eyes switched to Alex. "And who might you be?" His smile was a politician's—smooth, bland, and charming.

"Alex Ryan. I'm a friend of Megan's."

Almost imperceptibly, his face tightened as they shook hands. "Ah yes, Megan. Where is Megan?"

"Talking to the Walkings," Willy supplied, catching sight of the daughter in question.

He nodded. "You're new, aren't you?" he asked Alex.

"You mean like a gift?" She had decided to dislike him on sight. Her answer, though, startled a laugh out of him.

Megan, who had returned, overheard Alex's remark. Her eyes narrowed. "Hello, Father."

He nodded. "Megan. How are you?" he asked, his eyes scanning the room.

"I'm well."

"How is the store doing?"

You don't care one bit, Megan thought, but years of training had her smiling politely. "Busy."

"Good. Good."

Incredulous, Alex watched the scene unfold. She had rarely seen two people more uncomfortable with each other. She looked at one then the other, then her eyes caught Willy's exasperated look.

He glanced at his watch. "Well. I should mingle." He looked at Megan for a beat, almost as if hesitating over saying something more, then turned to his mother. "I will catch up with you all later." His eyes flickered to Alex, then he was gone.

Megan watched him leave, her face suddenly sad. With a barely visible shake of her head, she turned and handed one of her two glasses to Alex. "Sorry I took so long."

"That's okay. I was enjoying your grandmother's remarks about fate."

Megan looked over at Willy and her smile was affectionate. "Fate? Are you reading your tea leaves again?"

Willy smiled. "Of course. It always pays to be prepared. Fate does a pretty good job of arranging things, but sometimes it requires a small nudge here and there." Her gaze caught sight of a woman making her way to the bar. "Oh. I see my friend Beatrice over there. The cow." She winked at both girls. "I must go say hello." She kissed both of them, startling Alex, then with a smile, she was gone.

Megan looked across the room at her father, who had joined a small group of well-dressed men. She hated these functions, hated the hypocrisy of it all—all those plastic smiles and air kisses, while they went on pretending they were not sleeping with each other's spouses. She had attended hundreds of such functions over the years, paraded out to project the right image of family. Until the fateful night when she had confronted her father and poured out her heart, finally telling him she was gay. His biggest concern then had been the possible effect on his political career. To say that he had taken her coming out hard was an understatement; it had turned him into even more of a stranger. Now she was asked to attend his soirées only when necessary. She went out of duty, mostly to make her grandmother happy. She sighed in frustration and loss.

At the sound, Alex turned to Megan and with a finger traced Megan's cheek. "Have we stayed long enough yet?"

Megan, who had jumped at the feel of her touch, smiled without humor. "We just got here."

Alex grinned. "Yeah? It feels more than long enough. Besides, I'd rather be somewhere else with you right now." She pulled an unsuspecting Megan out of the room before she had a chance to protest. They left quickly, without saying goodbye. That would have been unthinkable for Megan, but for Alex it wasn't. They rushed to the car like children let out of school early. Inside, Alex turned in her seat and looked at Megan. "Did you want to go somewhere in particular?"

Megan stared back, suddenly wanting Alex with a force that stunned her. *What would she say if I told her the truth? Would I scare her off again?* She shrugged noncommittally. "Not really. It would be nice to just spend some time with you."

Alex switched the car into gear and peeled out with a squeal of tires, pulling a laugh out of Megan. "You like jazz and martinis?" When Megan nodded, she said, "Then I know the perfect place." She switched the radio on and with careless ease, wove in and out of city traffic at a speed that had Megan's hands clenching white-knuckled to the dashboard.

That they arrived at their destination in one piece was a miracle as far as Megan was concerned. She turned to Alex. "Do you always drive like that?"

Alex turned with a grin. "Like what?"

"Like you're late for something important?"

"I am." She reached over and unclipped Megan's seat belt. "We are late for our martinis, aren't we? Why waste time in traffic?"

They had driven down to a small martini bar in Boston's south end where many of the gay population socialized. As was usual for a Saturday night, the street was filled with people hurrying in and out of the numerous bars and cafés that lined this popular section of town. Across the street, despite the biting cold, a small group of die-hards was gathered on the steps of the coffee house, sipping espressos while watching the sights. Inside the bar, the lights were dimmed, the jazz loud, and the crowd of mostly men, thick. Alex, followed by Megan, plowed in; with luck they found a small loveseat in the back.

"Would you like a martini?"

"Sure."

Alex fought her way back to the long bar that crossed the length of the narrow room. Megan watched her order. She couldn't place her finger on it, but there was something different about Alex tonight, as if a weight had been lifted from her shoulders. She felt the heat of the attraction deep in her stomach, and smiled at Alex as she returned.

"I come here for the olives." Alex grinned and popped one in her mouth. She lifted her glass and toasted. "Here's to making new friends."

Megan smiled. "Is that what I am?"

Alex looked at her thoughtfully, eyes very blue. "I'm not sure what you are."

Megan, who had been looking around, turned and met Alex's gaze. The look held for a moment, an acknowledgement of the feelings pressing down on them. Suddenly unable to breathe, Megan broke the contact.

Alex tasted her drink, savored the cold, smooth gin on her tongue. "So, what's between you and your father?"

Megan, who had recovered most of her good humor since leaving the party, smiled ruefully. "Oh, you noticed?"

"It's hard to miss."

Megan sighed. "Let's just say that I am a huge disappointment, and he never fails to remind me in countless ways."

"Why? What have you done that is disappointing?"

Megan took a long swallow, enjoyed the coolness as it inched down her throat. "I was born a girl. That was the first." When Alex continued to look at her expectantly, she smiled. "Do you really want to hear all of the gory details of my life?"

Alex looked at her, then away. "I'm interested in everything about you," she said quietly. Her eyes came back to her tablemate. The look was intimate.

Megan shivered. *Oh yeah. I'm in trouble.* She pushed her hair back in a careless gesture that had Alex aching to touch it, but her fingers circled her glass instead as Megan continued. "Well, let's see, beside the being a girl part, my father wanted me to become a lawyer, so to please him, I did." At Alex's look of surprise, she nodded. "Yep."

Alex made a face. "Lawyer."

Megan laughed. "I became one about three years ago. I did it by working my ass off. Graduated in the top 5% of my class. Passed the bar on my first attempt. Typical overachiever."

Alex whistled. "I'm impressed."

Megan grinned. "Don't be. I became a defense attorney." Alex looked so disgusted, Megan patted her hand with a smile. "Yeah, I know. We are a match made in heaven. You arrest them, I work to let them go." Alex shook her head. "But that's what he wanted. At that time, I would have done anything to make him happy. I still remember racing home after passing the bar so I could tell him." Megan looked down at the white tablecloth, remembering with faded hurt the day she ran into his private study beaming, eager for his approval. "All he said was to never again interrupt his work for something so trivial."

Alex frowned, remembering the smooth man at the party and wishing she could go back and knock him senseless. She smiled at her thought.

Megan munched on an olive, feeling the old hurt recede. So much time had passed, it felt like a lifetime ago. "I practiced law for two years, hating every minute of it. There were times when I would be in some boardroom discussing upcoming trials, and a little voice inside my head would be screaming 'Guilty, guilty, bring back the death penalty!' Then one day, at a low point in my life, I was out walking in Copley Square. I hated my job, my heart had recently been broken." She shook her head, her smile rueful.

Alex registered the quick jolt of jealousy for the woman who had broken it.

"I didn't know what I should do with my life. Then I looked up and saw a for sale sign in a window, and it was just like an omen." Megan grinned. "Willy is not the only believer in fate. That very day I went in and bought myself a bookstore. Then I walked into my father's study, told him I was gay, I was through being a lawyer, and I was now in the book selling business—all in one breath. He has barely spoken to me since. I still don't know what he took the hardest: that I'm a lesbian, or that I failed at the family business." At Alex's look of inquiry, Megan added, "Law is like a religion in my family. My father, grandfather, and great grandfather were all lawyers."

Alex shook her head. "Wow. That's quite the story. Don't you ever miss it?"

"What?"

"The law."

Megan smiled. "Sure, sometimes. Not enough to try it again, though. I love being surrounded by books. So, your turn."

Alex rubbed her chin thoughtfully. She felt none of the panic at getting personal this time. "I can't come close to that story." She grinned at Megan's interested look. "Okay, but first," she lifted her empty glass, "how about another?" At Megan's nod, she fought her way back to the bar. She could spend hours sitting across from Megan as she talked. Just watching that mouth, looking into those eyes. She smiled at Megan as she returned, felt the jolt of her perfume.

"My father never knew that I was gay. I mean, maybe he suspected, I don't know." She shrugged. "I was always his little buddy. I guess I was the son he never had. We would spend hours taking apart an engine or playing catch."

Megan's look was wistful at the words. *Family. That's how it's supposed to be.*

"He was a cop. He was killed in the line of duty when I was sixteen. Traffic stop gone bad." She frowned, remembering. "They never found the killer."

Pity flooded Megan as she imagined the teenager's devastation at the loss. She had been too young when her own mother died, barely remembered the woman who had fleetingly filled her life. She reached over and took Alex's hand.

Unconsciously, Alex turned her hand over and rubbed her thumb across Megan's knuckles. Megan felt the quiet touch all the way to her toes. "It was a long time ago. He died doing something he loved. Not many people can say that."

Her eyes were shadowed for a moment as she remembered the day her mother had opened the door to a pale chief of police and knew without being told that her husband was dead. Alex had stood at the top of the stairs, unseen by either of them. As she watched her mother collapse into the arms of the chief, she knew that her life would never be the same.

"I guess I decided to become a cop on the day of his funeral. They gave his badge to my mom, and I stared at it lying there in her lap and I knew then that I would be wearing it one day. And I am. I mean I did." *Did.* She frowned into her drink as the word caught in her throat, but then shook the mood off. "My mother is...what's the word I can use? A bit theatrical, to say the least." At Megan's amused look of disbelief, she nodded. "You'll see soon enough. Wait 'til you meet her. When I told her I was becoming a cop, she stopped talking to me and took to her bed for two weeks.

"She didn't fail to let me know what she was feeling about the whole thing by calling my sister every day to tell her I was ruining her life. She would call her at work and tell her I was giving her heart palpitations. Ashley decided right then and there that she had been born into the wrong family. For a while, she even fantasized that she was actually adopted." Megan started to laugh. Alex grinned back. "Then when I told my mom I was gay, she decided I was trying to put her into an early grave. There were more heart palpitations then, too. She believed that it was my way of rebelling against her authority, and 'Thank God my poor father was not around to see it. It would have broken his heart.' That went on for months. Until she saw some talk show and realized that having a gay child held some kind of prestige. She gets all kinds of attention from her friends now. Maybe because she keeps bringing it up as if she's some kind of authority on the subject. She moved to Virginia to be closer to her sister, and I've learned that I love my mother much more from afar." She shrugged.

Megan smiled at that. Alex smiled back, a smile that went straight through Megan, and she knew with a sudden clarity that was startling that she was falling in love. "I know I told you this before, Alex, but, you have a beautiful smile." The look they exchanged was quiet as they each accepted the attraction that was pulling at them.

Alex toyed with the idea of kissing her right then and there. "Can we go?" she suddenly asked.

Megan looked startled. "What? Oh, okay." They left the bar and ran to the car, the wind swirling white powder all around them.

They rode home in silence. Alex sped through the icy streets, fighting the urge to pull the car over and jump her. Megan, unaware of the struggle, puzzled over the abrupt ending to their evening. *I will never get this woman,* she thought, looking out of her window. *Never. Just when I thought we were finally connecting, getting close, sharing a piece of ourselves, something changed and she ran off.* Inside their hallway, Megan unlocked her door and turned to thank Alex for the evening. Her mouth was curled endearingly into the beginning of a disappointed pout.

Whatever she was about to say died on her lips as Alex's mouth descended on hers and shattered her to pieces. Megan fell back against the door as her mouth parted under Alex's. Someone groaned as tongue met tongue and body connected to body.

Alex's hand fisted in Megan's hair, bringing her mouth closer. Just as suddenly, she softened the pressure, her mouth gentling over Megan's, causing the blonde's knees to buckle.

She grabbed onto Alex's shoulders for support. When Alex tried to pull away, it was Megan who turned into her, grabbing her head to drag Alex's mouth to hers. She parted her lips with the wet tip of her tongue, tasting the dark mystery inside. Alex almost whimpered. Megan lifted her head and stared at Alex. Her heart had gone wild, the pulse in her neck beating a rapid dance.

"Stay with me tonight," Megan whispered. Her finger traced Alex's mouth. "Please."

Alex stared at Megan's flushed face, her green eyes dark and mysterious, that sexy mouth curving enticingly. *That mouth alone could drive someone insane.* She had to clench her hands to stop herself from ripping clothes off. Need, outrageous need clawed at her. She nodded, not trusting herself to speak.

Megan pulled her in and closed the door behind them. She threw her coat over the back of a chair and switched on a frosted glass lamp. It turned everything a soft golden color. She turned to Alex. "Would you like a drink?" A suddenly shy Alex shook her head. Megan held out her hand and pulled her close. She rubbed Alex's lower lip softly with her thumb. "I've been dying to do this all night." Megan's mouth descended and swallowed Alex's soft sigh, as her hand brushed the strong jaw line then trailed down Alex's neck, feeling the heat rise under her fingers.

Alex's eyes turned almost black as she felt the arousal pulse through her. It had been so long.

"Alex, I want you," Megan whispered, as her mouth followed the same pathway as her hand, to taste and savor her skin.

Alex made a sound deep in her throat and closed her eyes. *Oh no! I've forgotten how to breathe,* she thought, panicking.

Megan lifted her head to look at her as she felt Alex tremble. "Is this okay?"

"More than okay."

"Come with me." They held hands as they walked to the bedroom. Megan left her standing by the bed as she lit several candles around the room.

Alex watched the light dance on the wall and wondered if she would now wake up to realize she was having the most erotic of dreams. Megan turned back to face her, slowly undoing her blouse, letting it fall to the floor. Alex's mouth went dry at the sight of the pale skin draped in a whisper of silk. "You are stunning," she whispered.

"So are you." Megan took her hand and pulled her to the bed. She gently pushed Alex down and followed her, her body settling itself perfectly over Alex's.

Alex groaned. *We fit,* she thought, just before their mouths fused. Megan slipped a leg between Alex's, her chest rubbing erotically against Alex. Alex's hands found their way to Megan's back, enjoying the feel of her skin, memorizing the texture. Then her hand inched up to cup Megan's breast through the lacy bra. Megan moaned quietly at the gentle touch, her nipples hardening. Through the wisp of silk, Alex's fingers rubbed the hardened peak.

Then Megan's mind went blank as Alex pulled her up and closed a hot mouth over one of her nipples. Megan expected speed now, a rush to complete; but instead, the almost unbearably slow exploration continued. Clothes somehow got removed, bare skin met bare skin, and soft sighs and quiet purrs filled the room. Megan's mouth turned greedy as it trailed a heated path down Alex's body to close on one nipple. *Now*, her mind thought. *Now.* Then one hand went in search of heat...and found it. Found the silky wetness. She gasped. *How can I feel so much with just the tips of my fingers?* With the lightest of touches, she slipped her fingers in and pushed Alex over the edge.

Alex cried out and buried her face in Megan's neck, breathing her in, letting the shudders go through her. It was quick and sharp. *Mine*, she thought, before her mind emptied.

Megan, feeling Alex's body shuddering below hers, hearing her muffled cries, was helpless to stop herself from coming too. *That was unexpected.* "Alex." Her mouth found Alex's and she let the waves wash over her. They lay there, tangled up, breath shuddering, racing hearts slowing, until Megan lifted her head and looked at Alex, who still lay there with eyes closed.

"I can't see," Alex whispered.

Megan smiled and trailed soft kisses along her jaw. "Your eyes are closed."

Alex opened them and grinned. "Thank God! I thought I had been struck blind."

They looked at each other smiling, unwilling to break the contact. "Wow!" Megan said, slowly moving off Alex's body. She laid down beside her and took a deep breath.

Alex shifted and leaned on her elbow, head resting on one hand. "Wow back." One hand caressed Megan's neck, trailing along her ribcage, over her hip, then back up again to trace the soft curve of a breast. Her thumb moved over Megan's nipple, felt it harden in response.

Megan's eyes widened as she felt the familiar tingle between her legs. *So soon?* She closed her eyes when Alex's warm mouth closed on the tip. Alex sucked on it—lips, teeth, mouth toying with the nub until Megan moaned, her hands holding Alex closer.

Alex lifted her head and looked at her. "I want you again."

Megan opened her eyes and her mouth curved sensuously. "Is that right? Well, it would appear that the feeling is mutual."

Alex's hand reached lower to touch her. Her eyes closed with pleasure at the ready wetness she found. *This won't be enough.* Her fingers parted the swollen lips to slip in then out, rubbing gently with her thumb.

Megan shivered as the heat spread. Lips tangled, tongues met then retreated, murmurs were soft, indistinct in the quiet night. The moon was a sliver of pale light through partially opened blinds.

Alex stretched over Megan's body. With her fingers inside

Megan, she straddled Megan's thigh between her own aching legs. She drank in the pleasure flickering on Megan's face, watched her eyelids flutter closed, her mouth part on a moan as she brought her to the edge. She pulled back and watched Megan's eyes open, dazed.

Megan took a shuddering breath. "Alex..." she whispered.

"I'm right here." Alex took her time—nibbling her neck, savoring the taste of her skin. Her mouth traveled the length of Megan's body, exploring and tasting each inch then unhurriedly moving back up again. Finding with her mouth and tongue what pleased Megan. She returned to the tender skin inside her thigh.

Megan was almost mindless with pleasure. Her whole body quivered, looking for relief. *Please,* she thought, or maybe whispered it.

The soft moan drove Alex crazy. She usually would not have tried to be so intimate so soon with someone she barely knew, but she was driven with the need to taste Megan and to please her.

When Alex's tongue found her core and silkily slipped inside of her, Megan cried out. Her hands fisted in Alex's hair to hold her close. She felt Alex's tongue—quick and soft—dart over her, then back inside. "Alex, I'm coming," she whispered. There wasn't any way to hold back. She came almost immediately. This time it went on and on, and left her completely spent—weightless, unable to focus. For several minutes they held on tight. *So this is what falling in love feels like,* Megan thought as she drifted to sleep still wrapped in Alex's arms.

Alex watched her sleep, fingers unable to stop themselves from touching, exploring. She fell asleep holding Megan; and for the first time in months, slept right through the night.

SHE WOKE UP to the smell of coffee. Stretching, feeling the pleasant ache in her limbs, she smiled as the previous night came flooding back and with it, feelings she didn't want to examine too closely. Her eyes opened slowly and she smiled at Megan, standing by the foot of the bed with a mug of coffee. She looked ravishing in her bathrobe, tangled hair tumbling to her shoulders.

"Morning."

Megan walked over and held out her mug. "Coffee?"

"Mmm." Alex took a sip, savored the kick of caffeine.

Megan reached over and brushed a strand of hair from Alex's forehead. "How did you sleep?"

"Like a log." She sat up and the sheet fell to her waist.

Megan's eyes drifted down, heated, lifted up again. "Will you spend the day with me?" Megan asked, a hint of shyness in the question.

Alex looked at her, felt something fall, unaware that it was her heart. She nodded.

Chapter
Twelve

IF MONTHS EARLIER someone had told Alex she would love spending hours exploring dusty bookshelves, she would have laughed in their faces. But now, on her knees searching for a rare find, delighting in the tattered covers she discovered, she couldn't remember ever being happier. She wasn't in love, she was quick to tell herself, she was simply enjoying the thrilling adventure of romance with a beautiful woman. That was entirely different. If she were in love, she'd be worried. She would sit by the phone, waiting for Megan to call. Well, if she had a phone. And she would be thinking of her every minute of every day, planning every night around her. *None of that is true*, she decided. Well, maybe she did think of Megan at odd times, like now, but it was simply because she was here in the antique shop poring over books with her.

Megan—who had been in another aisle—found her grinning on the floor. Unable to stop herself, she bent down and kissed Alex's neck, startling her.

"Hey!" Alex looked up at her. "I found a *Winnie the Pooh*!"

"You did? Let me see." Megan looked at the book in her outstretched hand and smiled indulgently. "So you did. Lucky you. I've been searching for that one."

Alex's fingers traced the well-worn cover. "You can't have it; I'm keeping it."

"You don't even like reading!"

"So? Maybe I'm going to start. Anyway...finders keepers." She grinned.

Megan's fingers brushed through her hair. "Okay. Now how about some lunch?"

They found a small café inside a converted Victorian and, with luck, a table. The tiny room resembled an English parlor. They sat and, feeling the urge to linger, ordered wine. Megan watched Alex concentrate over the menu. It had been six weeks since that amazing first night. And each day as they got to know each other better,

Megan fell deeper in love. She had yet to tell Alex, afraid of scaring her off. But Alex was already part of her life and she of hers, though neither of them seemed able to admit it. Cautious, they were still holding back from even mentioning the word "relation-ship."

She'd nudged Alex into cooking meals at home, even bought her candles and a plant Alex insisted she would kill. They went to the opera, and to a downtown festival—where Alex had sat through authors' readings without falling asleep. Alex had taught her to play pool, and had taken her to a hockey game and spent it watching Megan eat mustard covered pretzels. For some reason, the mix of styles and tastes seemed to slide into a perfect union. Megan had learned that Alex was incapable of conversation in the morning before coffee. Alex had learned Megan had an almost pathologic fear of spiders. And yet, it all meshed. Most nights they held each other in front of a fire and talked long into the night, marveling at how easy it all was.

After lunch they explored the quiet street, going in and out of antique shops and bookstores. Every opportunity to touch each other was taken. An accidental brush of hands as they walked, a quiet rubbing of shoulders as they stood a little too close over counters. At a Starbucks, they stopped and ordered coffees. Alex was grinning at Megan when she turned and her eyes collided with those of her former superior. He smiled as he crossed the room to her. "Hello there, Alex."

"Captain."

"You are looking well." He stood ramrod straight, silver hair gleaming. His face was hard, lines deeply etched; he looked intimi-dating. Until you looked into his tired eyes and saw the kindness there. "How have you been?"

"Good. Better." She was flooded with feelings, but unable to grasp any to examine them.

He smiled then, and with a gentle fist touched her chin. "You should drop by and say hello, Alex. We all miss you."

There was a slice of panic at the thought, but she nodded. "Maybe I will."

His smile was kind, then he turned and walked away. Alex stood lost in thought until Megan touched her shoulder, causing her to jump.

"Who was that?" Megan asked, curious.

"Nobody."

Megan looked at her for moment but decided not to pursue it. "Ready to go?"

Alex, looking thoughtful, nodded. They drove home in silence. Alex was pensive, battling the thoughts and emotion that had surfaced at seeing her former commanding officer. Sensing her pulling away, Megan glanced at her throughout the ride, trying to think of a way to break through.

Back at her door, Megan turned in surprised when Alex made no move to follow her inside. Instead, Alex had already unlocked her own door to go in. "Alex? Aren't you coming in?"

Alex turned, almost surprised to see her. "Uh...no. I...I have a headache. I think I'm just going to turn in and relax for a while."

Megan felt a quick stab of hurt. "Okay. Come by later if you feel up to it." Alex nodded absently and closed the door. Megan rubbed the ache in her stomach. Something had happened, yet she was unsure of what.

Chapter
Thirteen

MEGAN JUMPED UP as she heard the familiar footsteps outside her door. She crossed to the door and pulled it opened. "Hey!"

Alex turned. "Hey."

"Alex, can I talk to you?"

"I'm a little tired, Megan."

"Well, that's too damn bad." Megan crossed the hallway. For the past week she had tried everything to break through the wall Alex had erected. Every time Megan had tried to speak with the brunette, she was met with a laundry list of excuses, each one less believable than the one that came before.

Alex's eyes widened slightly at the aggressive tone, but with a shrug she stepped back to let Megan inside. Alex dropped her keys on the table and crossed to the kitchen. "Want a beer?"

"No." Megan clenched her teeth, fighting down the frustration and the hurt. What she wanted was to know what the hell had happened. How they could have been as close as two people can be, then be like strangers, was beyond her understanding. She took a deep breath and tried to stay calm, fighting off the icy fingers of panic.

Alex returned with a beer and took a long swallow. She lifted a brow at Megan. *Play it cool,* she thought. She had made a decision that she wasn't sure Megan would be comfortable with. She needed to test the waters first. More than anything, she didn't want Megan to be scared away.

Megan looked at her, saw the distance in her eyes, the faint arrogance in the unreadable face, and clenched her fists. *So this is how it is. She's dumping me.* Pride made her straighten her back, her green eyes turning cool. "I think I deserve an explanation."

"About what?"

"About what is going on. I haven't seen you in over a week."

"I do have a life outside of you, you know."

Megan's eyes flickered as she felt the blow. Anger replaced the hurt. "Well, that was a bit harsh. Is that the point? Are you trying to start a fight?" Alex did not answer. "Why won't you talk to me?"

"About what? There really isn't anything to talk about." *Not yet,* Alex thought. *Not until I can find a way to tell you about Sam and about why I'm going back.*

Megan stood on unsteady legs. *Well, that's that. I'm not going to beg.* "Well...I guess I know where I stand." All she had to do was cross the hall, then she could break down. She would not do it in front of Alex. Her pride sustained her as she crossed the room.

Alex fought down the panic. "Megan, listen...."

Megan turned, her face pale. "Alex, don't. I don't know what has happened, but I do know an ending when I see one. Let it go at that." As she closed the door behind her, she swallowed the tight ball of pain. Inside her apartment she dropped to the couch, her skin suddenly icy. She felt the pressure build behind her eyes, but she refused to cry. Not yet.

Stunned at the turn of events, Alex stood indecisively in her living room. *Well, that went well.* She charged out of the apartment. She tried Megan's door, but it was locked. "Megan?" She knocked on the door. "Megan, please open the door." Megan sat in the darkness and tried to ignore the pounding. "Megan! Open the damn door!"

Megan snorted. *So now she wants to talk. Well, it will be a cold day in hell...*

Alex wiggled the doorknob in frustration and strained to hear beyond the thick oak. She ran back into her apartment and found her keys. Fumbled for the right one, she let herself into Megan's place and peered into the darkness. "Meg?" She found Megan sitting on the couch, glaring at her.

Damn! I forgot about the spare. Megan stood up. "I want you to leave." She held out her hand. "And give me back my key."

Alex slammed the door shut and pocketed the key. "No."

Megan felt her anger break. "What the hell do you mean, no? Give me back my damn key."

Alex shook her head stubbornly. *No way. I'm not going anywhere.*

"Who the fuck do you think you are?" Megan yelled.

"A damn fool, obviously. Someone who keeps making stupid mistakes," she yelled back, stepping closer.

"I want you to leave, Alex." Megan took a step back.

"No you don't." Filled with admiration, Alex looked at her. She was beautiful when she was angry. She saw Megan clench her fist, and surprise made Alex recoil. *Would she really hit me?*

Instead, Megan turned away. "I don't know what kind of game you think you're playing, but I want no part of it." She disappeared into the kitchen and poured herself a glass of water with hands that were shaking. *Dammit. Damn her.*

Alex silently followed , slipped behind Megan and pressed up against her. Megan went rigid at the feel of Alex's body. The glass slipped from her fingers and shattered in the sink. Alex nuzzled her neck. "I'm sorry, honey." Her hands circled Megan's body to bring her close.

Megan turned, hurt in her eyes. "You're being a jerk."

"I know. I'm so sorry. I didn't realize..."

Still Megan held back. "Alex, what is going on with you? I never know whether you're coming or going. If what we are building isn't what you want, don't play games. It's unkind. And I don't believe you're cruel; so what is it?"

"Nothing." When Megan's body tensed, she drew back a little. "It's nothing you can help me with right now, honest. Just something I need to work through on my own. But, honey, please believe that it has nothing to do with you. I want to be with you more than I want to breathe, okay?" She kissed Megan, desperation and need surging through her.

Megan stood rigid, undecided, fighting against giving in. *I really will never understand her.* But the feel of Alex's eager mouth had Megan's whole body melting like hot wax as the need poured through her. She anticipated the violence of their mouths fusing together hard, and gloried in it. Her tongue plunged into Alex's mouth to tangle with hers. The hands that she had lifted to push Alex away instead clenched fistfuls of clothing to drag her closer. Something was unleashed in Megan that matched Alex's intensity. As much as she was scared by the barely restrained control, Megan thrilled under the passion.

Alex tore Megan's shirt open and buttons flew to the floor. Megan's eyes widened at that. She couldn't ignore the thrill she felt at being so wanted. They tumbled to the floor. Megan straddled Alex and pulled her sweater off, then her hands fumbled at the opening of Alex's jeans. "Take them off," she ordered, and Alex complied. Their mouths met again and again, hunger clawing just below the surface. "Look at me, Alex," Megan ordered as her fingers found Alex wet and ready. As Alex's eyes flickered open, Megan asked, "Do you want me? Do you want this?"

Alex's eyes closed at the unbearable pleasure. "Yes...yes. Now, baby. Please." Alex pushed up against Megan's hand, looking for relief.

Megan held her hand away ever so slightly. "Do you want to come?"

Alex groaned and her mouth opened wide. Her hands fought the last barrier of clothing and entered Megan.

Megan shuddered at the sensation. She fought for control, determined to make Alex want her as much as she wanted Alex. This time she would be the one making Alex crazy with need. Megan slid lower and replaced her hand with her mouth. She tasted Alex and took her time slipping through the wetness. Her tongue darted over, then slipped in deeply, and Alex felt the sensations race through her. She groaned. Her hands fisted beside her, she spread her legs wider. Megan's fingers joined her mouth and as her tongue circled the swollen skin, her fingers gathered the moisture deeper as she entered Alex.

Every thought, every sensation was concentrated in one area. Alex felt the heat grow and spread. Her heart pounded in her chest and she knew that if the house suddenly collapsed around them, she wouldn't be able to lift a hand to save them. She was completely helpless, her whole being focused on Megan's mouth and the unbelievable things it was doing. "Please...baby...please."

Megan lifted her head and watched Alex, saw the flush heat her skin. She studied with fascination the rapid beating of the pulse at the base of her throat. "Alex?" she whispered.

Almost mindless, Alex lifted heavy lids to look at her. The look in her eyes was one of absolute need, desire...and surrender.

Megan smiled. Then her mouth closed on her and she started to suck gently. Her tongue replaced her fingers and plunged in. Alex cried out as the climax ripped through her. It went on and on, and still Megan did not stop as she continued to suck and toy with the soft skin.

Alex's whole body clenched, almost in pain, and still that unbelievable mouth continued. *I need to stop her,* Alex thought, but her arms lay heavy on the floor. *I can't take anymore.* The second climax tore a scream from her.

Megan slid up Alex's body and gathered her close and held her tight until the shudders quieted. Her ability to pull that kind of response from Alex filled her with awe. She finally understood her own vulnerability towards Alex, as well. *This is where I want to spend the rest of my life.*

Alex's hand sought Megan's hand, then held it tight. "Are we still breathing?" Alex whispered.

"I think so."

"Oh, good. I think it's going to take me a year to recover my senses."

Chapter
Fourteen

"TYPICAL—LYING AROUND 'til noon. "

Madison heard the voice dimly through sleep, recognized it, and groaned. "Oh, Christ, go away, Alex."

"Nice to see you, too. " With apparent glee, Alex gave the drape cord an enthusiastic tug and sent sunlight lasering into her friend's eyes.

"I've always hated you. " In defense, Madison pulled a pillow over her face. "Go pick on someone else. "

"I dropped everything just so I could pick on you. " In her efficient way, she sat on the edge of the bed and snatched the pillow out of Madison's hands. Concern was masked behind an appraising eye. "You don't look half bad. "

Madison pried open one eye, saw the smile, and shut it again. "Go away. "

"If I go, the coffee goes. "

"Coffee? "

"Mmhm. And croissants. "

"Okay, you can stay. " Madison sat up and held out her hand for the cup of coffee. She took a long sip. "How did you know where I would be? " Madison asked after a moment.

Alex studied her a while. "Darcy called and told me you showed up last night and went straight to bed. " She didn't mention that she had also said that Madison had been hysterical and Darcy could not get anything out of her. Alex had come as soon as she could. She had asked Megan to come along, wanting her near.

"Want to tell me what happened? "

Madison sighed. "I messed up real bad this time. I have no idea how to fix it. " Alex continued to watch her, saying nothing. "I went and fell in love with Lauren. Madly, completely, hopelessly; and it makes no sense. And the worst part is, now she is pregnant. " Her eyes welled up and she started to cry. Alex hid her shock. Lauren—a well known television journalist—was one of Alex's closest friends from college, and a married woman—married to the senator from their state, no less. And, it now appeared, a mother-to-be.

I should have known something was up. For months Lauren had been evasive, Madison distracted. Even during her anti-social period, she had seen glimpses of that. She cursed herself for being so wrapped up in her own little world that she had missed the signs, missed being there for her friend. Still... *Lauren and Madison?* That was an idea that she would need time to adjust to. Her heart broke for them. She focused on Madison's crying.

"Hey, don't do that! " Alex said in a panic. Cool under pressure, she disintegrated in the face of tears. "I'm so sorry, honey. "

"I don't know what to do. I don't know how to recover from this. It's like waking up after sleeping for years and feeling everything more acutely, seeing everything so much brighter. The colors are more beautiful, the joy more intense, the pain more unbearable. I don't know how I can put the pieces of my life back together again. "

Alex stroked her head, her touch gentle. "I am so very sorry. "

Madison smiled sadly. "I'm in love with her; I know with absolute certainty that I'll never love anyone this much again. I just wish it didn't hurt so damn bad."

Alex reacted to the pain on Madison's face. Right at the moment, her shock at hearing about Madison's involvement with Lauren was tempered with her concern for Madison. Tomorrow, her concern and worry would be for the both of them, but it broke her heart to see her friend in such pain. She was and would always be a fiercely protective friend. "She doesn't deserve your love."

"I don't think that's for you to say."

"Madison, I know it hurts, but maybe this is for the best. She has not left her husband, and she is pregnant. That should tell you where her head is at."

"I hear what you are saying, but this is very different for her. And it has shaken her up just as much as it has affected me."

"How can you know?"

"Because a person can fuck anyone, but she loves only one. Me."

"You believe that?"

"I have to." The gray eyes swirled with images, feelings. "I have to..." she whispered.

Seeing her friend's evident agony arising from an impossible situation, Alex flashed to her own grief and pain over Sam, and then to her new feelings for Megan. She refused to put a label on those feelings, yet she couldn't help but wonder what she would be like if this new thing with Megan didn't work out. She shied away from thinking about it, turning to comfort her friend.

Megan, who had been standing silently in the doorway, glanced at Alex—who was about to speak—and frowned. The shake of her head was almost imperceptible; Alex stayed silent about her doubts about Lauren's feelings. "I'm so sorry, honey."

Later in their room, Alex turned to Megan. "Why did you shake your head at me?"

"Alex, I know you hurt for your friend, but she feels awful enough without having more pain piled on top."

"Wait until I talk to Lauren, I'll..."

"You'll do nothing." Megan's tone was firm. "You weren't there. You don't know what Lauren was going through, *is* going through. It's easy to sit in judgment, especially when someone we love is hurt, but we just don't know what really happened."

Alex sighed. *Megan's right. What do I know for sure?* "It's just that I've never seen Madison like this. It's like a part of her has died. She is so broken. Lauren should leave Matt. Hell, she should have left him years ago when she started to have feelings for another stupid girl. I mean, she has been unhappy for years; why the hell stay with the jerk?"

"Leaving a relationship is never easy, for a number of reasons."

Alex thought back to her time with Sam and stayed quiet. Megan had a point.

"Sometimes you can meet someone and it is never meant to last. The intensity of the feelings is too strong to survive. It burns too brightly. Maybe the fit is *too* right. Like—once you find your true soul mate, you can't survive it. I don't know. Life has a way of blowing up on people for a multitude of reasons, most of all when we love."

Alex hesitated. Here was the perfect opportunity to tell Megan about Sam and about what had happened. Megan's look was questioning, as if she could feel her struggle. Alex opened her mouth but closed it without speaking, unable to find the words. Fear held her back. She wasn't ready to be that vulnerable with anyone again.

"I'M THINKING OF going back to work."

Jamie turned. "Seriously?"

"Yeah. I realized that I miss it. Isn't that something? Despite everything that has happened, I miss it—every minute of the boring routine. Those endless reports, the smart-mouthed hookers, the endless hours sitting in a car." Since running into her captain, she had been overwhelmed by the feeling that she should be back at work. As a test, she had finally gone down to the downtown division to see everyone for the first time since the funeral. She had walked in and been assaulted by the smell of burnt coffee, cleansers, and too many unwashed bodies; and it had felt like home. She had missed it. It was time to go back.

"Hot damn!" Jamie smiled at her. "I never thought I would hear those words coming from you."

Alex grinned foolishly. "I know."

"What does Megan think about it?"

Alex's grin faded. "She doesn't. I mean, I haven't told her yet. It doesn't concern her."

"Doesn't it?" Jamie pursed her lips. She wasn't one to interfere capriciously, but this had disaster written all over it. "You should tell her."

"I will when I'm ready. I just need to figure out a way to tell her everything."

Jamie hesitated. "Sometimes the easiest thing is to start at the beginning. From what I can sense of Megan, she will understand and support you."

Alex shrugged. "I'll tell her. I just need some time to figure it out—how to tell her...about Sam."

Jamie sat down on the couch, her teeth worrying her bottom lip. *It's really none of my business.* She hesitated, but one look at her friend's face told her she wouldn't get anywhere anyway, so she let it go. "Are things good between you guys?"

"They're actually awesome." Alex smiled. "I mean, they couldn't be better. We had our first fight last week." Her eyes went dreamy, remembering how they'd made up.

Jamie grinned. "Is that right? Too bad. I was actually thinking of asking her out." She started to laugh at Alex's snarl. "Oh, baby, you have it bad."

"I do not," Alex defended hotly. "I'm just enjoying what we have."

"Uh huh." Jamie nodded. "You have it bad."

Alex grinned. "Maybe." At Jamie's knowing look, she threw a cushion at her. "Oh, shut up."

MEGAN REALIGNED THE display for the third time, then stepped back. She would deny being a perfectionist, but there were times when things needed to look perfect. She was preparing for her first author's meeting, and nerves had her rearranging every inch of her bookstore. She had fought hard to be taken seriously in the tiny, closeted world of independent booksellers. With patience and hard work, she had built quite a loyal clientele, and finally, after three years, her hard work had paid off. Finally, a famous author would venture into her store to read from her latest best-seller, to sign autographs and mingle with her buying public, and all because of hard work. She grinned. *Well, it did help that the author is gay and quite smitten with me,* she admitted to herself. She turned when she heard the front door bell ring out, and smiled as she recognized Andrew. They had met several times over the past few weeks, and had discovered a common passion for arcade games. She now considered him a friend.

Andrew grinned at her. "Hey there, beautiful."

"Hey there, ugly."

He swaggered over. "Whatcha doing?"

"Getting ready for an author's meeting."

He rolled his eyes. "Yuck. Brain food." He grabbed a book from the display, noting Megan's quick look of panic. He grinned. *It is so easy to get a rise out of her.* Then he whistled when he took in the picture on the dust cover of the book. "Hot. Maybe I should come over. She looks good enough to eat." When his eyes lifted, he caught Megan's amused look. "No way. She's not."

Megan nodded. "Yep. She's on my team."

He swayed comically. "You're breaking my heart." He frowned in mock anger. "Aren't lesbians supposed to be ugly?"

Megan patted his shoulder. "That's just a rumor started by a broken man unable to bear the truth." He put the book back in the wrong place; Megan did not notice. She had just decided that her display was still in the wrong spot after all. She grabbed his arm. "Come on, I need you."

After an hour of grunting and heaving, he had the display right where she wanted it, and he was sweating. "See, you do need a man around."

"I never denied it. Men are good to keep around to open jars and kill bugs, and, of course, to move really heavy stuff." He frowned at that. She laughed. "Come on, macho man, I'll give you a beer."

They made their way back upstairs. "Where's Alex?"

Megan shrugged. "Out. Visiting her sister, I think." Inside, she grabbed a beer for herself and handed one over to him.

"I thought I could grab a game of pool with her. When is she ever going to get a phone?"

Megan smiled. "Never. She likes playing hard to get."

He looked around the apartment and stepped closer to the bookcases. "That's a lot of books." He frowned at the titles.

Megan shook her head. "What is it about cops and reading?"

He turned, his face suddenly serious. "Speaking of cops, isn't it great news about Alex? I never thought she would come back after what happened to Sam, but I..." He broke off at Megan's look. "You didn't know?"

"No. Alex didn't mention it." She fought to work a smile onto her lips, but couldn't make it reach her eyes. "It's good news, though. No—great news. How long have you known?"

He hung his head. "A couple of days. I'm sure she planned on telling you herself. Once she, ah..." But he couldn't think of any excuses. "I'm sorry."

"Don't be, Andy. It's okay, really. I'm sure she will tell me." She turned mechanically. "I'm sorry, Andy, but I have to get back to work."

Andrew placed the bottle on a table and followed her out. At the front door, he turned, concern in his eyes. "I'm sorry, Megan."

She nodded. "I know. It's okay. Really."

ODD THINGS HAPPEN to the mind at two o'clock in the morning, particularly when waiting for a woman. The mind starts to worry, to project, to sweat and to speculate. Alex paced her living room floor. *Where the hell is she?* As she had many times over the past four hours, she strode to the back door and glared out. Her car was alone out there, as she was alone inside. *Damn woman.* She strode back to her apartment and stared at the clock. *Two-oh-one. Why wouldn't she have called?* Then she swore when she remembered not having a phone. *Maybe she had an accident and couldn't reach me.* She fought down the panic. *That's it,* she promised herself. *Tomorrow I'm getting a phone.* Then a fresh thought made her swear. *What if she is out with the babe from Maine, the writer who had the hots for her? What if right this second she is in some hotel room kissing her?* She spun around, the fury flowing through her, then stopped pacing when she heard the key in the lock. She was out of the door and into the hall before Megan had the front door fully open.

"Where the hell have you been?" The demand burst out of her, ripe with worried fury. "Do you have any idea what time it is?"

"Yes." Very deliberately, Megan closed the outside door and locked it. "Sorry. I didn't realize I had a curfew." She was able to walk past her only because Alex was too stunned to stop her.

Alex recovered quickly, caught up with her at the door of her apartment and spun her around. "Where were you?"

Megan jammed the key in the lock and shoved the door open. "Out."

Alex slapped a hand against the door before she could close it. "Alone?"

"Does it matter?" She took off her coat and hung it in the closet. "How I choose to spend my time is my business."

Jealousy was clouding Alex's thinking. She fought through the haze. "You have no right..."

Megan interrupted her, green eyes icy. "Don't you dare talk to me about rights." She walked past Alex and into the kitchen to get a glass of water.

"Megan, I was sick with worry."

"I'm sorry if you were worried. It didn't occur to me that you would be."

"It didn't occur to you? I was half- crazy with worry. I was about to call the police."

"Ah yes, the police." Her eyes were as dull as her voice. "I hear congratulations are in order, *detective*."

"It's not official until next week." Alex spoke carefully, studying Megan. She had seldom seen eyes that cold or that detached. "How did you find out?"

"Does it matter? It's more to the point that I didn't find out from you. Excuse me." She brushed past her and into the living room.

Alex closed her eyes and cursed herself for a fool. She followed Megan into the living room. "So you're pissed. Okay. But..."

"No," Megan interrupted. "It's not okay. And I'm not pissed." Because she was tired, unbearably so, she gave in to it and sat down on the arm of the sofa. "You could say I've been enlightened. You could even say I'm devastated. But no, Alex, I can't say that I'm pissed."

The quiet resignation reached Alex. "Megan, I didn't do it to hurt you."

"I know that. That's why I say I'm enlightened. You didn't tell me because you didn't think it was any of my business. You didn't *want* it to be any of my business is probably more like it. It was a major decision in your life. *Your* life," she emphasized, "not mine, or ours. So why bother telling me?"

Megan was slipping away. She was standing two feet away, but Alex could feel the distance between them growing by leaps and bounds; and it terrified her. "You make it sound as though I was keeping it from you. I needed to work it out, that's all. I was going to tell you, but I didn't think you would understand."

"You didn't give me the chance, Alex," she said quietly. "Did you really think that I could have felt what I did for you and not understood how important being a cop was to you?"

Her use of the past tense sent a fresh wave of panic skittering down Alex's spine. "Megan...I..." At the look in Megan's eyes, she stopped. It tore down all her defenses.

"Alex, I know you've had it rough." At Alex's questioning look, she sighed. "I know all about Samantha. I've known since the beginning."

"How did you..."

Megan shook her head. "Ours is a small community. Someone recognized your name from the newspapers and pieced it together. Don't you see? That's not the point. The point is—*you* never told me. Just like now. I know why you held yourself back at the beginning. At least I think I do. But you've been making your own choices for a long time. And one of those was in not letting me share your life. You chose not to accept my feelings for you, and you chose not to let yourself feel anything in return. And you know what? I *do* blame you for that." The hands in her lap were clenched tight. "I blame you very much for hurting me. I don't handle pain very well. And since you have broken my heart, I think you should know it."

"For Christ's sake, Megan..." Alex started toward her, but stopped when Megan jumped up and moved away.

"Don't. I don't want you to touch me right now." She spoke quietly, clinging to the slippery edge of control. "I really don't. It's humiliating enough for me to finally understand that sex is all we had."

"That's not true." Alex fisted her hands at her sides. "You're blowing this out of proportion, Megan. It's just a job."

"I wish it were, but we both know it's not. It's the most important part of your life. You gave it up to punish yourself, and you're taking it back because you can't be completely happy without it. And I just wish that you could have shared that with me, Alex." She turned, wrapping her arms around her waist protectively. "I wish you could have cared enough about what we had to tell me about the night Sam died."

"I do care about you, Megan."

Megan's eyes filled then, and she fought back tears. "You can't imagine what I would have given to hear you say that before. Just once, for you to look at me and tell me you needed me."

Alex felt helpless before the wall she'd put up between them. The hurt spread through her body. "What do you want now?"

"I'm going away tomorrow for a week. I expect that should give you enough time to find another place to stay, to move out."

"That's not the way to handle this."

"It's my way. And I figure I'm in a position to call the shots. I'm sorry, but I don't want you here when I get back."

"Fine." She had her pride. She'd been rejected before. She wouldn't beg. "I'll move out as soon as I can find a place." She turned to leave. As she reached for the doorknob, she realized that her hands were shaking and hot tears threatened. She turned, knowing with a sick feeling that she'd just been shut out of the best part of her life.

Chapter
Fifteen

SOMEONE HAD PUNCHED up a disgustingly cheerful seventies tune, and Alex considered, just for a moment, taking her gun from the holster on her belt and putting an end to the high-pitched voice that was wailing gleefully about an all-night party. She stared into her glass at what was left of her drink, and stifled the urge. *Good cops do not shoot jukeboxes.*

From a booth in the far corner, a woman laughed loudly. Without turning to look, Alex knew it was the skinny redhead who'd arrived shortly after her to meet two other girls. Gigglers all, but the redhead had a particularly irritating laugh. She sounded remarkably like Wilma Flintstone.

The bar was all but deserted on this miserable Tuesday night. It was usually packed on weekends, but on weeknights after ten o'clock it was quiet, a good place to be alone. Usually the weeknight patrons left the damn jukebox alone. The three giggling women in the corner, however, had been feeding quarters into it as if it were a slot machine. Alex didn't have anything against disco, but there was a time and place for shaking your bootie and tonight wasn't either.

She was at the tail end of a really bad day. Since leaving Megan's apartment building, bad days had piled up one after another. Her nerves were raw and jumpy, and the vodka and soda hadn't begun to settle them. She tensed as the door opened. She might be off duty, but that didn't make her stupid. She was alone, and there was no one there to watch her back. Her eyes drifted to the door. A lone woman came in, her eyes on the bartender. Alex watched with her peripheral vision as the blonde slid onto a bar stool, leaving two empty stools between them. Alex caught a glimpse of long, shapely legs and forced her eyes back to her drink.

"I'll give you five bucks to unplug that infernal machine," the blonde offered grumpily, waving a crumpled five-dollar bill at the pretty boy behind the bar. He gave her a brilliant smile, but shook his head. The woman didn't say anything else; she slipped out of a long cream-colored coat that was still sparkling with raindrops, and just placed her elbows on the bar and leaned forward to order a drink. Her hair was wet—not soaked through, but damp with dew-like moisture.

It's raining. Alex wasn't surprised. *A fitting end to a lousy day.*

Alex looked away as the woman tossed her coat over an empty bar stool. The blonde didn't say anything, just leaned on the bar, watching. The bartender was, as usual, efficient. She didn't have long to wait.

"Well." From behind the safety of the bar, Benny the bartender grinned brightly and planted himself between Alex and the blonde. His face was tanned, his teeth were white and his dark hair was moussed into a stupor. "I don't think I've ever seen two more miserable people in all my years as a bartender."

Alex was not impressed. *All his years? He's no more than twenty-five.*

The newest patron sipped her drink through a straw but paused long enough to respond to Benny's comment. "I've had a really bad day."

"Me, too," Alex mumbled, toying with her glass. The woman shot her a glance between sips, clear hazel eyes—set in a classically pretty face—drilling through her, looking at her and into her. The effect was immediate and powerful. Alex felt the jolt of it, and her mouth went suddenly dry. The eyes reminded her of Megan's, and she frowned. "Really bad," Alex added, as if to justify herself.

"I got a speeding ticket. Damn cops." The blonde licked the froth off the rim of her glass.

Alex winced. "Ouch." She wasn't going anywhere near that one.

"And I was fired," the blonde said as she attacked the straw again. She played with her strawberry daiquiri, swirling the straw through the frozen mix, lifting icy clumps on the end of the straw and watching them plop back into the glass. Finally she released the straw and swiveled to face Alex. "If I hadn't been doing my job, I would understand; but to be fired because the boss's new fiancée needs a job...well, that hurts. He said I was late one time too many, but I don't buy it." Alex answered with a noncommittal hum. "And my car's making a funny noise," she added.

"What kind of funny noise?" The blonde made a harsh gurgling noise that made no sense mechanically speaking, and Alex shook her head. "I don't know much about cars, but that sounds like a five hundred dollar noise."

She nodded mournfully. "That's what I thought." She shook her head in disgust. "Then to top it off, I got home to find ten mes-

sages. Ten! On my machine, all from my mother. She wants her
only daughter—that would be me—to get married. She wants
grandchildren before she's too old to bounce a baby on her frail old
knee. I get this every time one of her friends has another grand-
child," she said, grasping the straw with her restless fingers. "She
still doesn't understand why I broke up with my last boyfriend,
even though it's been over a year. She somehow thinks it's all a
cruel joke I perpetrate just to piss her off. John—the guy I dated
and the boss who fired me today—the same. That toad," she muttered under her breath.

Despite her gloom, Alex was entertained by the saga. She
shook her head knowingly. "Messy."

The blonde leaned forward. "So, what about you?"

Alex shook her head.

"Come on, I shared."

Alex grimaced. "I don't share. Ever."

The blonde sighed and drew away from her, distancing herself
physically and mentally. "Sorry," she mumbled. "Now don't I feel
like a complete fool? I unburden myself to a perfect stranger..."

"Detective Ryan's not perfect," Benny interjected.

Alex threw him an exasperated look, and Benny moved down
the bar. Alex swung her stool so she was facing the woman who'd
had such a bad day. "I almost killed a man today," she said softly.
The rage still burned low in the pit of her stomach. The woman
looked at her but said nothing. Alex hesitated. *Hell, maybe I need to
talk about it.* "I had to recover the bodies of two boys from the Bay
today. They were still in their pj's. Boys of about two and four."
Alex's jaw clenched and a muscle twitched in her cheek. "They
were drowned by their father. You know the reason he gave me for
the so-called incident? His new girlfriend didn't like children."

The woman looked horrified. Alex rubbed a hand across her
face and noticed, not for the first time, that her hand was shaking.
"I went after the bastard. I took my gun out and shoved it inside his
mouth and almost pulled the trigger." She didn't add that the only
thing that had stopped her was the flash of memory of all the blood
around Sam's body the night she was killed. She grimaced. "It
would have been too easy on him."

"Oh." The blonde nodded as if she understood perfectly. "You
win," she said as she lifted her half-empty glass in salute.

"What's the prize?" As soon as the flippant question was out of
her mouth, Alex regretted it. The blonde waved an elegant hand to
Benny indicating that this round was on her. Alex scooted over one
stool and so did the blonde. Their knees brushed, and they both
repositioned themselves quickly.

"Kate Vaughn," the newcomer said when she was comfortably

seated on her new perch, and she offered her hand.

"Alex Ryan." As their fingers slid together, the jukebox started up again. "I thought disco was dead," Kate said with a forlorn sigh.

It was a little late for second thoughts, but Alex knew she really shouldn't drink any more. She did feel better, but she wasn't sure if it was the drinks or the shared misery. The two months since she had moved out had been some of the worst times of her life. Missing Megan was like a physical ache—dull throbbing through every pore. She had never known anything like it. And it was worse because she knew she was to blame. She could not fault Megan for the breakup; it had all been her doing.

As good as her word, she had moved her stuff out and into Jamie's place. And then she had thrown herself into her work with a vengeance. She was like a woman possessed. No case was too small. So what if she thought she would go mad if she stopped working? And when she stopped sleeping, she told herself that sleep was overrated anyway. She was okay. She obviously wasn't in love with Megan. And if she found herself reaching for Megan at night, that was just a bad habit she needed to break. When she found herself driving over to Megan's, she chalked it up to just checking up on things. That's why she was a cop, wasn't it? For hours, she sat in her car staring up at the house. It gave her no comfort to know she had turned into a stalker.

She took another sip of her drink and forced her attention back to Kate. They dismissed their problems for a while by coming up with a few inventive and destructive ways to disable the jukebox. The ladies from the corner booth left, with the jukebox still playing. Kate made a face at their retreating backs.

Alex frowned into her drink. *Just my luck. They fed so many quarters into the machine, it might just play all night.*

The place was uncomfortably empty without the chattering women they'd listened to all evening. Kate played with what was left of her drink. The ice was melted, and she was just on the other side of tipsy. She didn't want to leave. What did she have waiting at home? She loved her house, but there was nothing—no one— waiting for her there. There were just messages from her mother...and a little harsh reality. She was in no mood to face either at the moment. She looked over at Alex, who looked gloomy again, as miserable as she had been when she'd just arrived and seen her there staring into her drink. *Maybe she doesn't want to go home either.*

They hadn't talked about her day since she'd described what had happened, but it had to be on her mind. She touched Alex's hand, startling her from her thoughts. For a moment as Alex's eyes lifted to her face, Kate stopped breathing. *What the hell was that all about?* Kate shook her head, trying to clear it. *Maybe I'm more drunk than I thought.* "You know, sitting there you look so lost—like you've lost your best friend."

Alex's laugh was short and without humor. "That, too." She pushed her drink away. "It's been a bad month. I was dumped too, a few weeks ago."

Kate smiled. "Oh, well, there you go—winning again."

Alex accepted the unexpectedly dry humor with a laugh and a shake of her head. "You remind me of her a bit," Alex said quietly.

"Her?" Kate raised a brow.

"Yeah." It had slipped out, and now Alex waited for it—the rejection, the pulling away. None of that appeared, only the quiet look she had come to recognize.

"She must be quite something."

"She is. I was a fool."

"Do you believe in fate?"

"No. But someone I know does."

Kate slid from her stool and swayed slightly as the alcohol played havoc with her balance. "I do. I believe that things always have a way of working out the way they should. Goodnight, Detective Ryan. Thanks for sharing your bad day with me." Alex mumbled something; Kate thought it sounded like "Anytime," but she couldn't be sure.

Kate didn't really want to go home, back to the emptiness and the messages from her mother, back to the reality of her life. She had no job and, strangely, felt like she was at a crossroads in her life—uncertain of her next move. When she came out of the restroom, she was surprised to find Alex, leaning against the wall by the pay phone with her head down and her hands in her pockets—waiting for her. As the ladies' room door swung closed, she lifted her head; and when their eyes met, Kate's heart skipped a beat. Alex Ryan had cop's eyes: eyes that had seen too much and never missed anything. *How could eyes like that be anything but lonely?*

"I can't let you drive home," Alex said softly.

"I walked. I wanted to show my good-for-nothing car that I didn't need it. My house isn't too far from here. I don't think it took me twenty minutes to get here."

"I'll walk with you," Alex offered. "I need the air to clear my head before I drive."

They started to walk along the street, their footsteps echoing on the pavement. In the distance, a siren wailed. Alex heard the rain before she felt it—fat drops that spluttered on the sidewalk and her shoulders and Kate's coat. Suddenly, she had to laugh. This was too predictable. Her life was turning into a bad B movie.

Alex took Kate's hand and they ran through the rain, back the way they'd come to the nearest cross street. Raindrops fell soft and plentiful over and around them as they ran. They could barely keep their eyes open against the pelting, and as they turned the corner, there it was, its red neon light flashing garishly in the night.

The hotel had been in Boston for a hundred years. It had once been elegant, perhaps even as recently as thirty years before. Today it was just two steps up from a dump. But it was close, and the rain was coming down harder. In the distance, thunder rumbled.

Alex pushed the door open and pulled Kate into the lobby, intent on waiting out the storm. The lights were too bright, showing off the faded and worn spots on the mismatched chairs and the wrinkles on the clerk who stood behind the desk.

To his credit, the old man didn't even look surprised to have two late-night customers stumbling in, sopping wet. The smile faded as his eyes lit on the gun on Alex's belt, then turned to obvious suspicion when he noted the badge. "I don't know nothin' about nothin'," the old man said as Alex stepped to the desk.

"Good for you. I want a room."

The clerk narrowed his eyes and looked from one woman to the other. His frown changed into a leer and he pushed the old-fashioned leather guest book forward slightly.

For a moment as her eyes took in all the Smiths and Jane Does registered, Alex wondered what went on in the old hotel. Her reliable gut instinct told her there were probably any number of illegal activities taking place above her head at that very moment. But she wouldn't be there long enough to worry about it. Drying off and sobering up was the plan. She signed her own name. Whatever was going on would still be going on tomorrow night, and the next, and the next.

The elevator lurched to a stop. They were stationary for what seemed like forever. "Tomorrow," Kate said softly to herself, "I take the stairs."

Inside the room, Alex tried a light switch. The room was faded and old and out of date, but it was also clean and utterly charming. Kate turned with a smile. "This is a wonderful room."

Alex looked at her. "You're soaking wet." Something flickered in the hazel eyes, and Alex's mouth went dry.

"I know. So are you." Kate crossed the room to her and stood very close, watching her searchingly. "Tell me, Alex Ryan, what does it feel like to kiss a woman?"

Alex closed her eyes for a moment. *God give me strength. I should have seen this one coming.* She swallowed, suddenly nervous. "Wonderful. Soft. Like nothing I've ever felt like before."

"Oh." Kate's eyes touched on her mouth and her lips parted.

Alex toyed with the idea of kissing her. *Why the hell not? Why not forget my bad day or month by spending some delicious hours making love with a beautiful woman? She obviously is curious.* Then Kate tossed her hair in a manner reminiscent of Megan, and Alex felt the pain clench her stomach muscles.

Kate seemed to feel her struggle as she took her hand. "Come on. Why don't we take off our wet things, lie down, and wait out the storm. I really don't want to be alone tonight."

"Me either," Alex whispered. Kate took off her shoes and wet stockings and pulled the covers down. Alex stripped off her wet shirt, carefully laying down her gun within reach.

Kate glanced at the gun but said nothing. They slipped in under the covers, and Kate suddenly was nervous. *What the hell am I doing? Alone in some grungy hotel room with a complete stranger. A cop, maybe, but still... A gay woman, no less. Boy, can I pick them.*

Alex looked at her and suddenly smiled. "Relax, Kate. You're safe with me."

Kate's eyes locked on hers and held. "That's what I'm afraid of." She smiled at herself ruefully. "This has been quite the day," she added.

"Quite."

"Well, it was nice to meet you, Alex Ryan." Kate turned over and slipped an arm around her pillow. The alcohol making her head swim a little, she was asleep in minutes.

"Likewise." Alex closed her eyes to rest just a moment and wait out the storm, and was soon passed out.

Kate didn't dream at all. She slept a deep and complete sleep. When she woke, she didn't open her eyes right away. She was warm; her body had burrowed into a comfy place in the soft mattress, and the arms around her were snug and secure. *Arms?* She opened one eye and found herself staring at a woman's softly curved chest. Bits and pieces of the previous night came back to her, enough for her to know who the woman beside her was, at least—Detective Alex Ryan, fellow hater of disco. *I've made a lot of mistakes in my life, but this one was a doozy. Exactly what happened last night?*

Alex was still sound asleep, and Kate watched her. Asleep, she looked years younger—the tension was gone, the inviting mouth soft. It wasn't a beautiful face, but it was striking. Without the incredible eyes, she was almost resistible. Almost.

Her eyes traveled along the lean body, stopping at the flat stomach. Her fingers suddenly itched to touch, and she felt heat suffuse her. *What's going on?* At any other time she would have recognized her body's reaction as lust... *But for a woman?* That was so very unexpected and scary. *I have to get out of here before I make a fool of myself.*

Very carefully, Kate extricated herself from Alex's hold. She sat up, trying not to rock the mattress any more than was necessary. Her head pounded. *I will never drink again,* she swore to herself as she dressed quickly. *Never. Not even so much as a sip.* At the door she hesitated, then crossed back to the bed and kissed Alex. "Thank you," she whispered. She didn't know exactly what she was thanking her for: for spending the night talking to her and helping her forget her bad day; for not coming on to her, or for understanding her loneliness. She tiptoed out.

Chapter
Sixteen

ALEX DREAMED OF jukeboxes and blondes and great legs all wrapped up in Megan. The disco pulse became irregular, punctuated by beats as intrusive and annoying as the familiar voice calling her name.

Alex opened her eyes and rocked into a sitting position. Her eyes peered at the clock. Almost seven. She looked around and realized that she was alone. For a moment, disoriented, she thought she had dreamt it all. The drumbeat—a furious pounding on her door that echoed in her aching head—continued, as did the voice calling her name. *My name?*

"Just a damn minute," she shouted, realizing too late that shouting was not the way to go the morning after. She wanted to throw the door open and glare at the person on the other side, but she had to satisfy herself with opening it slowly and glaring with one eye open and the other firmly closed. "What the hell do you want?"

She expected Jamie to make a joke, but her face was serious. Too serious. Her gray eyes looked past Alex to take in the contents of the room. "What's up, Jamie?" Alex backed away from the door and let her partner into the room. "How did you find me?" Alex glanced toward the bathroom, wondering if her pager was vibrating as they spoke. Then she remembered that she'd turned it off before going into the bar the night before.

"I didn't expect to see your name in the guest book of this dump, Alex," Jamie said accusingly. "You want to explain to me what you're doing here?"

Alex tried to think of a simple way to explain the night that had passed. *I met a woman in a bar, and we both hated disco...* But she couldn't say that. *It was raining...* Also no good, since her car was just a few blocks away. "No."

Jamie waited, her eyes glancing at the bed, noting the dents in both pillows. She turned to watch a now-dressed Alex strap on her gun belt. "I went to three bars last night, all the usual places, looking for you," Jamie said accusingly. "No one had seen you since you left the station. You turned your cell phone off. I almost went to Megan's to see if you were there."

Alex's heart stuttered; she looked horrified. "You didn't..."

"No, I didn't." Jamie frowned. "I was worried about you, Alex." She didn't tell her that she had also gone to the cemetery to Sam's grave, worried that the incident with the drowning of the children earlier in the day might have pushed Alex over the slippery edge of control.

"I'm a big girl, Jamie. I don't need to check in with you on an hourly basis just because I've had a bad day." The facts of that bad day came back and her eyes hardened. "I can take care of myself."

Jamie smiled without humor as she surveyed the room again. One brow lifted. "No doubt. Tell me about the woman you were with last night," Jamie said in a soft voice.

"What do you want to know about her?" Alex asked calmly. She was not even surprised to know that Jamie knew she'd had company. She had always been a good investigator.

Jamie walked to the window and threw back the drapes, letting horribly bright sunlight into the room. She smirked as Alex swore at the brightness. "I didn't know you were seeing anyone."

"I'm not."

Jamie took a deep breath. "Well, I don't know how to tell you this, other than to just come out with it. The handyman found a body in the stairwell an hour ago. A woman in her late twenties, early thirties, maybe. Blonde hair. No ID."

The shock pounded into Alex's chest and brain, and for a minute she couldn't breathe, much less speak. *God, not again!* Finally she stood slowly. Blonde hair. There was bound to be a number of blondes in the hotel; it could be anyone. Still, her heart thudded rapidly.

Jamie continued. "There's no handbag, so we figure maybe it was a mugging that went bad. The killer got her throat clean and deep with a very sharp knife. Tom says whoever cut her got her carotid artery so she lost consciousness just a few seconds later. She was dead within minutes." Jamie's voice was gentle, almost consoling.

"Alex," she continued softly, "the desk clerk thinks it might be the woman who came in with you last night. I hate to ask you to do this..." Alex knew what was coming. "We need you to take a look."

All Alex could think about as she followed Jamie down the long hall past the elevator were Kate's words as she'd stepped into that very hallway the night before. 'Tomorrow, I take the stairs.'

She tried to prepare herself for the worst as she followed Jamie down a flight and a half of stairs. She was thoroughly sick of death, sick of dealing with scum and the squalor of life. The air in the stairwell was stale with an underlying stench that wafted from the corners. *A lousy place to die, and I brought her here. It was all my fault. Again.*

Alex saw the blood first, a splash pattern that shot across a step at the bottom of this flight. Her hands started to shake as she took in the blood. The smell was too familiar and she paled, pulled back into a dark alley. She caught a glimpse of blonde hair curving across the concrete, lying obscenely close to a pool of blood. Feeling faint, she clenched her teeth; then as she focused, she realized the hair was longer, darker. *It's not Kate.* She sighed with relief. "It's not her," she said. "It's not her."

Jamie looked at her then nodded to an officer nearby, and they escaped the coppery stink of the stairwell. Outside, Alex gulped in great big breaths of air. Jamie looked at her with concern. "So, you want to tell me what happened last night, Alex? Do you always pick up women in strange bars?"

"Yeah. All the time." Alex gave her a give-me-a-break look. "Look, Jamie, it's not important. Nothing happened. It was just misery loving company. You wouldn't understand." They crossed to Jamie's car.

"Nothing happened?"

"No. Nothing."

"Was she at least pretty?"

"What the hell difference does it make?" Alex asked, annoyed.

"Just curious. Seeing if you have lost all grip on reality."

"I think she was pretty."

"You think? How drunk were you?" Jamie turned the key in the ignition. She didn't wait for the answer. "Well, at least you weren't parked in front of what's-her-name's again. Now *that's* pathetic."

Alex glared at her. The look that intimidated most people failed to even dent Jamie. "Go to hell."

"Whatever. Listen, kiddo, go home. You definitely need a day off. Get some sleep."

"Jamie, somebody killed that woman right under my nose, and I don't like it. Kate left the hotel..."

"Kate?"

"Shut up. According to the coroner's estimation of the time of death, Kate must have left the hotel around the time the murder occurred. Last night she said she would use the stairs. There's a good chance she might have seen something. I think we ought to talk to her."

"We? What's this 'we' business? It's *my* case," Jamie countered.

"We." Alex repeated with a smile. "She knows me."

"How well?" Jamie shook her head. "Never mind. Let's go, then. Where does she live?"

Alex leaned her aching head back and closed her eyes. "I haven't the faintest idea."

KATE FELT ALMOST human again. Two cups of coffee and a long hot shower had almost done the trick. She had even almost accepted the fact that she no longer had a job. She had enough money in her bank account to see her through several months with no problem. She also knew that she was good at her job. Computer programmers were in great demand, if she still wanted to be one.

She looked around the living room. She loved her little house, but it was in desperate need of some TLC. Maybe this unexpected time off was a blessing. She could finally tear down the wall between the living room and the kitchen and then... The sudden knock at the door interrupted her thoughts. She opened the door and froze at the sight before her: Alex Ryan. And she looked grim.

"Kate..."

She slammed the door in her face. A muffled laugh came from the other side of the door, a bright joyful laugh that she knew wasn't Alex.

Jamie glanced at Alex. "You've sure got a way with women," she said under her breath. Alex ignored her.

Kate rested her forehead against the closed door, the thought belatedly that she shouldn't have slammed it in Alex's face. The cop probably thought she was a basket case, a lunatic. She should really open the door again. The knock came again, softer than before. Kate took a deep breath and opened the door slowly; and this time she saw Alex was not alone. Another woman, another cop, she knew without bothering to look for the badge, stood just behind her. She was taller than Alex by a few inches. Short blonde hair was pushed back from her face.

This time, Alex stuck her foot in the doorway so Kate couldn't shut it again. "Hi, Kate. We need to ask you a few questions."

She looked puzzled. "I haven't done anything wrong..." *Except go to a motel with a cop in a middle of the night and have lustful thoughts about a woman.*

"Miss Vaughn," the other woman said as she nudged Alex out of the way, "you're not in trouble. No trouble at all." Kate looked into the gentle gray eyes and relaxed slightly.

As she spoke, Jamie tried to keep her tongue inside of her mouth. She hoped the drool wasn't visible. "I'm Detective Jamie Saunders. We hate to disturb you, but there was an incident this morning at the Bayview Hotel and we're questioning everyone who was there."

"Oh." She opened the door wider and stepped back. "How did you know...?" Then her eyes caught Alex's and she blushed. *That was stupid.* "Come on in. I've got coffee."

They stepped into the house. "None for me." Jamie smiled.

Kate's eyes widened. *Good God. That smile should be illegal.* Her hands pressed against her churning stomach. *I am just one big walking hormone these days. I have been without sex for way too long.*

"I'd kill for a cup," Alex mumbled appreciatively. "Black."

Kate jumped. She had forgotten Alex was there. Then she felt guilty, though she had no reason to. For sneaking out while Alex slept? For being at the hotel with her in the first place? For wanting to kiss her? Grateful for the excuse, she fled to the kitchen.

Watching her walk out of the room, Jamie turned with a meaningful look. "You *think* she was pretty?"

"What? Well, I was drunk." Alex shrugged. In the sober light of the morning she could tell she was pretty, and didn't look like Megan at all.

"And nothing happened?"

"What is this preoccupation with my sex life?"

Kate returned with a steaming mug of coffee. Alex accepted it gratefully and took a long sip. "Have a seat," Kate said, motioning to the sage-colored sofa. Jamie smiled and sat, withdrawing a small note pad from the pocket of her pants. Alex lowered herself slowly.

"What time did you leave the Bayview this morning, Miss Vaughn?" Jamie asked.

"Please, it's Kate."

"Kate." They exchanged a look that had Alex rolling her eyes.

"A little before seven." Jamie made a note.

"Did you take the stairs?" Alex broke in. Jamie glanced sideways at Alex, annoyance on her face.

"Yes."

"Did you see anyone?"

Kate took a deep breath. Her mind hadn't exactly been clear as she'd made her getaway, and she had to think for a moment. "A man in the hall changing a light bulb." Mentally she took the trip again. "A woman on her way up, between the first and second floors," she added, thinking for a long moment. "I ran into her, literally. She was running up with her head down, and I was running down. We collided. We spoke for a minute, then moved on."

Jamie's head lifted from her note pad. "Describe her, please."

Kate noticed the dark ring around Jamie's pupils. At first she had thought that her eyes were gray, but that wasn't quite it. They were smoky, like having someone look at you through a campfire.

Then she shook her head, knowing she had lost track of the question. "What? I'm sorry. I'm a little slow this morning. Lack of sleep."

Jamie shot Alex a look. Alex lifted her hands up as if to ward off the unspoken accusation. "Can you describe the woman you ran into?"

"I wasn't paying a lot of attention." As she'd made her way down the stairs, her only thought had been to get out of there, far from thoughts she had no right thinking. Or did she? *Well, I can't really say that.*

"It's important, Kate," Alex said softly.

Kate closed her eyes and tried to remember. "She was pretty. Tall, skinny, like a model. Long blonde hair. I think she was wearing a blue dress. It might have been green." Jamie and Alex exchanged a look. "What's going on?" A hint of worry crept into her voice.

"When you collided, what did she say?"

"She apologized and so did I, and then she asked me what perfume I was wearing."

"She what?"

"She asked me what perfume I was wearing 'cause she liked it."

"And you told her."

"Yeah, why not?"

"Anything else?"

"No."

"Was she carrying anything? A handbag, a suitcase, anything at all?"

"No, not that I could see." She grew more and more intrigued as the moments and the questions passed. "What happened? Did she do something?"

"No, she..."

"Hold on, Alex," Jamie said, a hint of warning in her voice. For some reason, she wanted to spare this woman the gory details. She kept her voice soft. "A woman was murdered this morning at the Bayview. From what we can tell, she was killed about the time you left. The woman you ran into on your way down matches her description."

It was clear from Kate's expression that whatever it was she had been expecting, it was not that. "Killed?" She paled. "My God!"

"We might need you to look at some photographs of the victim to confirm it is the same woman you saw."

Alex stood up. "You okay?" Kate looked at her and nodded.

"Kate, did you see anyone else on your way out? The desk

clerk, anyone?"

She shook her head. "Well, there was a man by the elevator. I don't know if he was coming or going. I didn't really pay attention."

"What did he look like?"

"Young, I think. Tall, fit. Blond. I'm sorry; his back was turned." She turned, agitated, and missed the look the two officers exchanged.

"Okay." They prepared to leave. "Listen, if you remember anything else or need anything, call me." Jamie handed her a business card after scribbling a phone number on the back. "This is my home number, just in case."

Alex smirked. "Yeah, here's my card too. In case you can't reach her." Her face was bland, eyes innocent, as Jamie stared at her.

"Oh. Thanks." Kate took both cards and threw them a puzzled look. She could feel the undercurrent of something, but she didn't know what it was.

Inside the car, Jamie turned the key. "She saw the killer."

"I would say so."

"The question is—did he see her?"

"Yep."

"I think I might put an extra patrol around her house just to be safe."

"Wise." Alex leaned her tired, aching head back against the headrest.

"Are you sure you didn't sleep with her last night?"

"I did sleep with her. That's all that I did."

"You are gay, right? I mean—you did see what she looked like? Weren't you even a bit tempted?"

Alex sighed. "Yeah. Last night, after several vodkas, I thought she looked like Megan, and I was tempted."

"Megan! She looks nothing like Megan."

"So I've noticed."

There was such dejection in her voice, Jamie reached out to touch her hand. "Honey, why don't you call her?"

Pride stiffened Alex's resolve. "No."

"Is she gay?"

"Megan?"

"No. Kate."

Alex closed her eyes. "No. But I think she is curious."

"Damn! I have a rule: never go after a straight woman." Jamie drummed her fingers impatiently on the steering wheel before turning the key in the ignition.

Alex groaned at the pounding in her head. "Yeah? Well I have a new rule: never talk to another blonde again. Never. Ever. You're all bad for my health."

Chapter
Seventeen

MEGAN CALCULATED THE invoices for the sixth time that day. The numbers still didn't add up. She frowned when Willy broke into a song as she dusted the bookshelves. *Must she sing all the time?* she thought. At the sound of the door opening, she pushed the papers away in disgust. *Damn it!* Then she looked up and her heart stopped as Alex's eyes looked back at her. No. The shape of the face was all wrong; it wasn't Alex. But the woman had the same deep blue eyes. She felt her heart lurch, then settle. "Hello."

The woman smiled a little uncertainly. "I was looking for Megan."

Megan mustered a smile. "I'm Megan."

The woman rushed forward, a wide smile on her face. "I'm so happy to finally meet you. Alex talks about you all the time." At Megan's blank look, she blushed. "Oh, silly me. I'm Ashley, Alex's sister."

They shook hands, then Megan introduced Willy. Ashley smiled at the sprightly white-haired woman. "Alex talks about you all the time, too."

Willy beamed. "Does she, now? How sweet! Isn't that the sweetest thing, Megan?"

"Quite," Megan managed between clenched teeth.

"I've been dying to meet you." Ashley looked embarrassed. "I'm not usually so nosy, but you've made quite an impact on my sister." Again she blushed.

Megan frowned.

"Is she here? I've been trying to reach her for days. I just wish she would get a phone..." At the look on Megan's face, she stopped.

Megan straightened and took a deep breath. "Alex moved out."

That startled Ashley. "She did? When? Why?"

"Two months ago." *Two months, 4 days, 6 hours and 45 minutes to be exact,* Megan thought.

"But why?" Ashley shook her head. "I'm sorry, I don't mean to pry, but..." She shrugged, at a loss for words.

"It didn't work out." Megan moved around the counter, ready to show her to the door.

"Would you like a nice cup of tea?"

That stopped Megan in her tracks. She threw a frustrated look at Willy, who cheerfully ignored her.

Ashley glanced uncertainly at Megan. "I wouldn't want to..."

"Nonsense. I was just brewing some." Willy hustled away, a germ of an idea forming in her mind.

They stood awkwardly. "You're very beautiful," Ashley said softly.

"Thank you."

"I mean, Alex told me, but I thought, 'Well, she's in love...'" At the look on Megan's face, her voiced trailed off. "I really don't mean to pry; it's just that I have never seen Alex so happy..." Ashley's hands twisted together and she turned in relief as Willy came bustling back in.

"It's been a long time coming. When our dad died, Alex took it the hardest. She was devastated. She stopped talking for weeks." Ashley accepted the cup with a smile. "I think the reason she became a cop was so that she could find his killer. Subconsciously, I think every man she arrests is the murderer."

Megan moved restlessly. She didn't want to hear anything about Alex. She certainly didn't want to start feeling sorry for her. She was barely surviving the days without wanting to break down every time she thought of her—which was constantly.

"Then when Sam died, I know that Alex felt responsible. Like she had failed again at being able to protect the people she cared about. Then she met you, and it was like I was rediscovering my sister again. For that, I have to say thank you."

When Megan didn't comment, Ashley glanced uncertainly at Willy, suddenly feeling awkward. *I always talk too damn much.* She placed her cup on the counter. "I should be going. I have wasted enough of your time." At the door she turned. "It would have been really nice to get to know you, Megan."

As the door closed Megan turned, frustrated. Willy clucked. "Megan, love, come have some tea."

Megan walked over and absentmindedly took the offered cup. She choked as the potent brew burned down her throat. "Are you trying to poison me?" she coughed out.

"No, just fortify you for what needs to be done."

"What is that?"

Willy smiled gently as she touched her cheek. "Love is not

easy, child. Only people we truly love can hurt us and disappoint us. That is what makes love so worthwhile. The rewards of loving and of being loved back are a miracle, a gift."

"She shut me out too many times, Nana."

At the childhood nickname, Willy smiled. "Child, you were always so worried about rejection, I think you just latched on to the first excuse you could find so you could be the one doing the rejecting."

Megan whirled around angrily. The comment struck too close to home and left her feeling defensive. "That's not true. I just got tired of battering at her defenses. Every wall she put up, I had to tear down—brick by brick. It got exhausting."

"Did you ever tell her how you felt?"

Megan shrugged impatiently. "Not really. But she should have known." Saying it out loud made her feel foolish. She frowned at the possibility that she had contributed to the lack of communication too.

Willy touched her cheek. "How? She's not a mind reader. By not being honest about your feelings, you might have shut her out just as effectively as she did you. She has known loss, too, child; and loving you terrifies her just as much, I'm sure. I think you might be asking too much of others when it comes to love. There is no such thing as perfection. Everyone makes mistakes." She did not mention Megan's father, but the message was clear. Angry and miserable, Megan turned and walked out of the room without another word; in her mind she knew Willy was right. Unperturbed, Willy watched her go. She had faith in her granddaughter.

"HOW ARE YOU?"

The concern in Lauren's voice washed over Alex, and she shook her head at the friend who had stopped in unexpectedly to check up on her. "You are just too much. You know, there is no justice in this world. You are the most spectacular-looking woman I know, and because there is no God, also the nicest. You should pretend to be a bitch once in a while," Alex finished with a smile. Lauren rolled her eyes.

"Seriously, Lauren, I should be asking how you are, not the other way around." She was alluding to Lauren's recent miscarriage and her break-up with Madison. At first, her concern had been for Madison's emotional state, but it had taken only one visit with Lauren to see that both of her friends needed her support. They were both suffering.

Lauren smiled, but it never quite reached her eyes. "I'm good. More interested in you at the moment."

Alex grinned. "Well, see, you and I will probably start an argument now over who goes first with their story of woe." She raised an eyebrow. "I'm worried about you, Lauren. You've cut yourself off from all of us. Don't think I haven't noticed you pulling away. And it's a good thing that you stopped in, because despite all that is going on with me, I still have enough time left to worry about you. I love you and Madison, and worry about you both."

Lauren made a face but did not comment. When their eyes met, Lauren looked away. Alex sighed at the pain evident on her friend's face; it mirrored what she saw every time she looked at Madison. Not for the first time, she thought about how relationships wreaked havoc on the people involved. No one in their right mind would want to be in one. Alex still didn't understand why Lauren had not followed her heart when it was so obvious how much she loved Madison. Husband be damned.

"One of these days you are going to have to ask yourself if going through the motions is enough of a reason to get up in the morning," Alex said gently.

Lauren paled slightly at the blunt words and finally asked, "How is she?" Since leaving Madison, Lauren had never mentioned her name, and everyone had tacitly gone along with the evasion.

Alex looked thoughtful, wanting to be kind. "Surviving. Hurting. Just like you. Just like all of us. But she is not alone. We are here for her, just like we are here for you. She has us to fall back on, but so do you. Even all the way from Washington."

"Well, same goes." Lauren fixed her golden eyes on her friend. "So, you didn't answer me. How are you?"

"Me? Never better." Alex's smile was ironic. "I'm much better at analyzing everyone else's problems; I suck when it comes to my own." Her eyes briefly turned dark with pain.

"You should go talk to Megan."

Alex had to smile at that. "You know, Jamie keeps saying the same thing."

"That's because we are right. Stop being so stubborn. Go see her."

"What about you? How about using some of that advice on yourself?"

Lauren smiled. "One heartbreak at a time, my friend."

Chapter
Eighteen

WHY IS THERE never anything decent on television at two in the morning? Alex channel-surfed, searching for something even remotely entertaining—a bad movie, an old sitcom, anything. Two hundred channels and nothing on. She ended up flipping between infomercials about car wax and spray-on hair.

Jamie was at a party, and though Alex had been invited, she had declined. She was in no mood for company. Her thoughts bounced between wondering what Megan was doing and the Bayview murder. There hadn't been a single defensive wound on the blonde's body, not so much as a scratch. Either the killer had taken her completely by surprise, or she had known her assailant and had thought she was safe up until the moment he cut her throat. Alex was inclined to dismiss the theory that the attack was random. Her instinct told her the blonde had known the person who had killed her. They still had no murder weapon, and so far their only witness—if you could call her that—was Kate.

KATE WASN'T SURE what woke her. Still disoriented and more asleep than awake, she'd rolled onto her stomach when she heard the noise again. It was no more than a scrape—a shoe across the hardwood floor, a drawer being opened and closed. It didn't belong there. Her heart lurched and every muscle in her body tensed. Someone was in the house.

She slid quietly from the bed to the floor, hiding in the shadows. What should I do? If I head for the door, I might run into the intruder. If I stay here, I might be trapped. Crouching by the bed, she carefully lifted the telephone receiver and silently prayed that the trespasser wouldn't hear her speak. She had left the cops' business cards by the bed, and she hurriedly dialed the first number.

"Alex?" she whispered. "There's somebody in my house."

"Megan?"

"No, it's Kate. There's somebody in my house."

Alex's voice was clear and alert. "Have you called 9-1-1?"

"No. Alex, someone is here." Her voice broke. "I'm calling from my bedroom." She heard Alex bark out commands. When she was done, she came back to her.

"I'm on my way, Kate."

"No! Oh God, please don't leave me." Panic was welling up.

"Kate..."

"Please don't leave me." Kate hated the desperation in her voice, but she was more terrified to feel alone.

"Okay. The police will be there soon." Her voice was quiet, comforting. "And as soon as they get there, I will hang up and make my way over there, okay?"

"Yes," she whispered, leaning against the mattress and closing her eyes. Then she heard it again, the soft scrape, but this time closer. Her eyes flew open and she held her breath. She saw the shadow first, a long shadow blocking the light from the bathroom. He was just outside her door. She was trapped.

The figure of a man came into view, and somehow he knew right where to look for her. His face was hidden behind a stocking cap with crudely cut holes for his eyes and mouth. With a gun in one hand pointed steadily at her, he stooped to take the phone wire in the other.

"No," she whispered, and he yanked forcefully at the cord, ripping it from the wall jack. The phone went dead.

"Where is it?"

"What?"

"Where is it?"

Kate took a deep breath. If she panicked, he would kill her. "Where is what?" she asked calmly, but her voice shook, betraying her fear.

"Make this easy for both of us," he whispered. "Just give me what I want and nobody else gets hurts."

Kate huddled on the floor. "This is a mistake. I don't know what you want."

He advanced menacingly but suddenly his head swiveled, hearing what her frozen brain had also just recognized. *Sirens!* While he was distracted, she gathered her courage and pushed past him, running out of the room. He grabbed for her; she felt his hand close on her t-shirt and heard the ripping sound it made. By now the adrenaline had kicked in, and she pulled away and ran down the stairs, intent on only one thing—making it outside. The sirens were louder, and she wondered if he would simply aim and shoot. She heard a sharp crack. Not pausing to wonder if he was firing, she wrenched the front door open.

She saw the cars pull in, sirens blaring, and crumpled down onto her front steps, her legs unable to carry her further. Her head dropped into her hands, and she started to shake.

A young officer ran to her. "Ma'am?"

"He's in my bedroom." But now that reaction was settling into her bones, the words came out incoherently. She waved toward the house and the officers took off running. Her head lifted at a screeching of tires and she watched, momentarily puzzled, as Alex came running toward her. She had forgotten calling her.

"Kate, are you okay?" Alex was almost beside herself. Kate's simple "no", followed by the abrupt dial tone, had taken years off of her life.

Kate stood up, trembling, and the concern in Alex's eyes was her undoing. She started to cry.

Alex wrapped her arms around her. "I'm here. Everything's okay."

One of the uniformed officers came out, looking disappointed. "There's no one here. But the patio door was open." He looked at Alex. "We didn't call for homicide."

"Did you search outside the house?"

"He's long gone..."

"Search it." Alex's command brooked no hesitation. They took off at a run. "Kate?" Her voice was gentle. "Can you tell me what happened?"

Kate had herself under control now. She was suddenly embarrassed by her crying jag and wiped her eyes dry. "I'm sorry. I panicked. Someone broke into my house. A man. His face was covered and he had a gun..." Alex's face hardened at that. "He kept asking me for something, like he thought I had something. God, I was so scared."

Alex touched her face, soothing. "I know. It's over."

"Please don't leave me."

Alex caught the quick shake of a head from the returning officers. *Nothing.* "I won't."

It had taken a while, but Kate was finally asleep in her bedroom. Alex watched her sleep for a while, then tiptoed out. She reached Jamie from her cell phone. "James?"

"Where are you?"

"Kate's."

"What? Are you kidding me?"

"There was an incident tonight. Someone broke in looking for something. My instinct's telling me it's all related to the Bayview and the dead blonde."

"I'll be right over."

"No, it's okay, Jamie. I'll stay and watch tonight. You can take tomorrow's shift."

"Uh, Alex..."

"Nothing's going to happen, Jamie. I swear. I'm not even remotely interested."

She meant it. Her mind was still too full of Megan to even think about anyone else...though there were times when she was tempted to just lose herself in someone, just for the release of it. She dropped down on the couch and leaned her head back. *I can't think about that now.*

Her thoughts drifted to the woman upstairs. *Kate. How is it that this woman I've known less than thirty-six hours has given me two of the most frightening moments of my life?*

The intruder had been looking for something, and that worried her. The dead blonde had possibly had something that someone had killed for, would still kill for. But there had been nothing near the woman, nothing in her pockets. Could she have lied to whoever killed her? Told him that Kate had whatever it was that was missing, as a way to buy time? If that was the case, Kate was still in danger. *But how would the bastard have known who Kate was? It doesn't make sense.* She went back to the bedroom to look in on Kate.

She jerked slightly and her eyes snapped opened, as if she'd awakened from a bad dream. Her eyes settled instantly on Alex; she smiled, and her eyes drifted closed again.

Damn, Alex thought, *I hate being needed.*

KATE BUSIED HERSELF with mundane cleaning, trying to keep from looking over at Alex, who had settled herself at the kitchen table, feet propped on a chair and making herself at home. Alex had spent most of the morning on the phone, and she'd been doing more listening than talking. She took notes, a scribbled mess that Kate had no way of deciphering when she glanced over her shoulder to study the page. Kate emptied the dishwasher. As she put away the mug, Alex stood up and stretched.

"We'll have the guy before you know it. I promise."

"And then you'll get out of my kitchen?" Kate smiled. Alex smiled back and Kate's insides did an unexpected little flip-flop. *Oh, she should smile more often.*

"Maybe."

The doorbell saved Kate from saying anything stupid. Alex moved past her and went to the door.

Jamie didn't appear to be at all surprised to see Alex answering the door. "I've got those photos," she said, waving a short stack of stiff Polaroids. She threw a smile at Kate when she saw her hesitating behind Alex. "Hi, Kate. I hear you had a bit of excitement here last night."

"To put it mildly," Alex muttered.

Jamie ignored her as she took in the slow blush on Kate's cheeks. She raised an eyebrow at Alex, then pushed past her. "You wouldn't happen to have some of that coffee now, would you?" she asked hopefully.

"Sure."

Once Jamie had her caffeine infusion in hand, she looked at Kate for a beat. "We would like you to take a look at some photos." She pulled up a chair and motioned to Kate.

Kate suddenly felt like she was no longer in control of her life. She sighed at the insistent look on Jamie's face. *Fine; if she wants me to sit down, I will.*

"Is this the woman you ran into the other night?" Jamie asked, placing a photo on the table in front of her.

Kate glanced down. This particular photograph had been taken in a morgue or funeral home. The body was lying on a steel bed, and there was no blood or visible wound to be seen. A sheet covered her to her chin, and she looked almost like she was sleeping. Except that her face was white, and even her lips had no color left.

Kate touched the photo with one hand. It was hard to match the cold, lifeless figure in the picture to the laughing blonde who had accidentally run into her at the Bayview. Someone had purposely taken a life. This life. This was the closest she had ever come to having death touch her. She wasn't sure what to feel, except pity for the young woman who would no longer worry about mundane things like what perfume to wear.   "Yeah. That's her. Does she have a name?"

Jamie scooped up the photo and added it to the stack. "Yeah. Her name is Monica Webb. She was a hooker."

Her voice was devoid of any expression, but Kate detected something in her tone and lifted interested eyes to her.

Jamie looked back at her calmly. "Good coffee." She turned to Alex. "Find out anything yet?"

Alex, who had been leaning against the door frame, straightened. "Not yet. We are looking into her business dealings—regular johns, usual spots." She watched Jamie watch Kate and hid a smile. "Well, I guess I'll be off..."

Kate stood up, alarmed. "What? Are you leaving?"

"Don't worry, Kate, it's my watch tonight," Jamie answered with a smile. Kate threw her a quick glance and her heart skipped a beat.

"Oh. Fine. That's just fine." It wasn't fine at all. *If she smiles at me a few more times, I'm sure to do something embarrassing.*

Jamie gently nudged Alex out of the kitchen. "Come on, Detective Ryan. I'll see you to the door."

At the door, they faced each other. "Well, James, be good, I guess. Remember your rule." Alex grinned.

"Yeah, well, rules were meant to be broken."

"Careful, Jamie. She's a witness. Don't tamper with the evidence."

"Tampering would be nice, but don't worry. I will be on my best behavior."

"Call me if anything comes up." Alex descended the steps.

"Alex?" Alex turned, one eyebrow raised. "Megan was at the party last night."

Alex's face closed up. "Yeah?"

"She wasn't alone." She didn't add that Megan looked miserable, but her eyes were watchful as she studied her friend. The silence was telling.

Alex felt the punch of that settle in—a swift kick of heat she didn't want to acknowledge. Then she shrugged and made to turn away.

Jamie stopped her. "You should talk to her before it's too late."

"It's already too late."

Frustrated, Jamie glared at the departing car, worried that her friend's stubbornness was demanding a high price.

BY EVENING, KATE was a basket case. Jamie had settled herself in the kitchen in the same spot as Alex had and spent several hours on the phone. *Must be a cop thing*, Kate thought. She felt unnerved by the constant reminder that someone wanted to hurt her. And feeling Jamie's eyes follow her as she walked around was putting her on edge. Abruptly, she turned and headed for the doorway. "I'm going to take a bath," she muttered, then felt the frustration of having to announce her every move.

As if sensing her mood, Jamie barely looked up from staring at her notes. They had nothing. What were they missing? Every good homicide cop knew the majority of evidence was collected in the first twenty-four hours after a murder. That time had elapsed, and they still had little to go on. Another trip to the Bayview might be a good idea.

Restless, she stood up and walked into the living room. Her eyes touched on the computer and the modem. She was tired of speaking on the phone and considered checking some more files from work, via the computer. *Best ask if it's okay.*

She knocked softly on the door and, not hearing anything, peeked in. Seeing the bathroom empty, she entered, and approached the connecting door. "Kate?" She stepped into the bedroom and stopped in her tracks. Kate was standing beside the bed undressing, a robe in her hand. "I'm sorry." Jamie's voice was husky.

Kate, surprised, watched with fascination as the slow flush spread over Jamie's face. Their eyes met and Kate saw an awareness and a longing that floored her. She had never felt so turned on. She slowly let the robe drop and watched as Jamie's eyes took her in.

Jamie felt on fire, her hands clenched at her side. "I wanted to ask if I could use your computer to dial in to work." She turned quickly. She hadn't meant for her voice to sound so rough.

"Sure, go ahead," Kate replied softly.

Jamie fled the bedroom and stumbled back into the living room. *She is a witness,* Jamie admonished herself. *Get a grip.* But her eyes peered back toward the bedroom, and her teeth clenched as she remembered the sight of Kate's body. *Good God!*

Kate slowly bent down and picked up her robe. She felt the heat between her legs as she moved. She didn't understand what was going on, but whatever is was—she didn't want it to stop.

Chapter
Nineteen

THE BAYVIEW HOTEL looked even worse by daylight than it did at night. Every chipped brick, every suspicious stain and winding crack in the sidewalk screamed dump.

Alex and Jamie stepped into the lobby and faced a different clerk than Alex had the last time she'd been to the Bayview. The woman was as wrinkled and openly suspicious as the old man who'd been working there that rainy night. She watched the two of them through narrowed, pale eyes, a cigarette dangling from puckered lips.

Alex flashed her badge. "Mrs. Carson, I would like to ask you a few questions."

The old woman leaned against her counter. "All I've been doing is answering questions." Her voice was raspy from too many years spent chain-smoking. Her rancid breath curled Alex's stomach.

"Well then," Jamie interjected with a smile, "a few more won't be a big deal."

The old woman sighed. With her steel-gray hair pulled back into a tight bun and her shapeless, flowered polyester dress, she looked like someone's grandmother—a sweet old lady who should be baking cookies and drinking tea. A flash of Willy's face filled Alex's mind for a moment. But this was no grandmother. Her face betrayed the harshness of living on the edge for too many years, mapped as it was into weary creases.

"The girl who was murdered paid cash," the old woman said. "Received no visitors that I know of in the three days she was here, and she signed her name as Jane Doe. No," she said tiredly, "I did not ask for ID, no, I did not see her driving a car, and no, I did not see her with anyone else at the time."

"Thank you," Alex said, leaning against the counter. "I just have a couple more questions." The old woman glared at her. "Were there any other unusual guests here the same time as Jane Doe?"

The old woman cackled. "Just you, Detective Ryan, and your girlfriend. My husband thought it was a hoot that there was a detective sleeping upstairs while the murder was taking place." She coughed once, then again.

Alex did not think it was funny. Her eyes narrowed.

Jamie laughed. "Yeah. That's very funny. Cracks me up every time." Jamie reached out and snagged the leather guest book, and before Mrs. Carson could so much as complain, she flipped through a few pages. "Oh look, Jane's brother John was staying here," she said, pointing at a floppily scrawled "John Doe." "And damn near the entire Smith family it seems. Bob, Joe, little Billy."

Looking over Jamie's shoulder, a name caught Alex's attention, and she reached out and flipped the page. Her stomach clenched as she read the scrawled signatures, and she quickly glanced over at Jamie to see if she had noticed them, but Jamie was too busy glaring at the old woman as she slapped the book shut. "Do you have any customers who sign their own names?"

Mrs. Carson wasn't intimidated. "Just Detective Ryan."

Alex had had enough. She leaned forward slightly and lowered her voice. "You know, if we can't get the answers we want from you, we might just have to knock on every door in this dump. Your clientele seems to come and go with great frequency, so we might have to come back every night for—oh, what do you think?" She looked over at Jamie. "A couple of weeks?"

Jamie smiled. "At the very least."

Finally the old woman was worried. "I won't have no business left."

"Probably not."

Mrs. Carson straightened her spine, but there was a hint of reluctant surrender in her eyes. "She's been here before."

"Jane Doe?"

"Yes, Jane Doe," the old lady snapped. "Except the other times, she wasn't Jane Doe. She's one of my regular guests." She scratched at her double chin. "I do remember that a few months ago, she was starting to get a female visitor." She glanced at Alex and smirked. "I figured she was servicing both sides, you know?"

Alex ignored the jibe. "I don't suppose you got a name for that visitor?"

"She didn't sign in."

"Was she a hooker, too?"

The old lady frowned. "I don't ask their profession when they come in. I respect people's privacy." Her tone held censure. She lit another cigarette with the dying butt of her previous one. She took a long drag and pushed the smoke out through her nostrils. "Actually, I thought she looked too classy to be one of them working girls, real lady-like. Blonde, and dressed real clean."

"What about her last male visitor? The one last week?" It was too much to hope for, but Alex had to ask. "Sam Spade."

"Sam Spade?" Jamie rolled her eyes. "Like in *The Maltese Falcon?*"

The old lady shrugged. "Hey, I didn't ask. But I'd recognize him if I ever saw his face again. He was a purty one. Blond. Tall, like a movie star, you know. He was dressed real sharp. At first I thought he was one of you guys. He walked like one."

"A cop?" It wasn't much, but it was better than nothing.

Chapter
Twenty

KATE WAS MAKING coffee when the phone rang. Even though it was after nine, she was groggy and still half-asleep. Through the night, she had been too aware of Jamie in the other room to sleep. The sun had been coming up when she'd finally succumbed to exhaustion.

The caller ID was working, and she smiled when she saw Ryan on the display. "Hello."

"Well, good morning," Alex said. "Is James up and about?"

"No, she's still asleep."

"What? Wake her up. This isn't a vacation."

Kate left the receiver on the counter. She'd peeked in at Jamie earlier and saw her sprawled across the too-small couch, dead to the world. She had fallen asleep in her clothes. She didn't wear her gun, of course, but it was on the table, close at hand. "Phone." Jamie didn't stir. She raised her voice slightly. "Jamie, Alex is on the phone." Nothing. She crossed the living room to shake her gently, laying a hand on the arm that crossed her chest. As soon as she touched her arm, Jamie came awake, her eyes opening slowly and one hand drifting sensually over Kate's. Jamie's fingers closed one at a time, as she took Kate's hand and held it gently.

Eyes more asleep than awake looked at her with such longing that for a moment Kate was tempted to lean over and kiss her. Maybe it was just what they both needed. "Some watchdog you are," she said softly. "An entire army could tramp through here and it wouldn't disturb your sleep." Jamie came instantly awake and bolted upright, releasing her hand. "Phone." Kate backed away. "It's Alex."

THE NAMES WERE nagging at her like an ache just under the skin, impossible to get at. She was missing something, but what? After touching base with Jamie, Alex dialed a number from memory. "Jack? It's Alex. I need you to do me a favor. Can you run a check on a Caucasian male last known as Chris Billings?" She waited as he wrote it down. At his question she said, "No, nothing specific; just trying to tie up some loose ends in a case I'm working on."

Her fingers drummed impatiently against the steering wheel as she waited. Finding Chris Billings' name on the registry of the Bayview had been a surprise. With it had come a quick slice of pain as her mind threatened to revisit the last time they had been face to face, with him on the business end of her gun muzzle. But even worse, seeing the name just below his had been like being hit over the head. She had recognized the unreadable signature. Hadn't she called it a squiggly for years? She just couldn't make sense of things yet.

He came back on several minutes later. "He's got half a dozen priors—mostly drug related, small time robbery stuff. He operated out of the Bayview." There was a pause as he typed in a few keystrokes. "He's deceased as of last June when..." His voice trailed off as he read further. "Alex? Isn't that the guy..."

"Yeah, yeah," Alex interrupted him brusquely. She didn't want to talk about it. It had been the first time in ten years as an officer that she had fired her weapon outside of the shooting range. The memory, if she went there, still stung. She had killed someone. The fact that she had enjoyed doing it, had tasted the revenge in her mouth, still made her shiver.

The Bayview. It just confirmed that it was his name she had seen. It wasn't much, if anything at all. *What am I missing?* It kept tugging at her. She was about to thank him and hang up when his next words stopped her. "You know the weird thing is, all of his arrests were made by the same cop. Strange coincidence, huh?"

"Do you know who the cop was?"

"Yeah, I got a badge number." There was a pause as he flipped through his papers and then hit a few keys. "5812."

Alex thanked him and then threw the phone on the seat next to her. *5812. Something about that number sounds familiar.* Her hand reached for the key, and just as she was about to turn it in the ignition, it came at her with a searing flash. *Damn!* She didn't even know why she wasn't surprised.

She drove back to Jamie's and went searching through her stuff, realizing too late that what she needed had been left back at Megan's. In her rush to move out she had left a couple of boxes behind, intending to pick them up at a later time. She sighed. *Things can never be easy.*

Coffee, a shower, and a change of clothes later, Alex stood alone in Jamie's living room. She had changed into a tight, navy blue t-shirt and loose-fitting beige pants that hung low on her hips. Unable to settle, she paced around the room. *What if I'm wrong?* She stopped pacing. *What if I'm right?* There had to be an explanation. She was probably reaching for answers. *This could just be one big coincidence.* Except, she had never believed in coincidences. Especially when they piled in one after the other.

She needed a break—a break from Jamie, from thinking about their investigation, a break from the creepy thoughts about Sam that were starting to crowd in on her. She wanted out. On impulse, she grabbed her keys and left without leaving a note. She started driving without any particular direction in mind. The fact that a couple of hours later, she found herself parked in front of Megan's place was hardly surprising. She sat in the car and stared up at the brownstone, missing her, undecided about her next move. *Now that I'm here, what can I do?*

WHEN MEGAN GLANCED through the partially opened blinds, she did a double take. *Is that Alex's car?* She peered closer and could swear it was. Heart hammering, she pulled back and waited. *Maybe I'm mistaken, but what if I'm not?* She peeked out again. The car was still there. She could make out someone in the driver's seat, but not their features. When the car showed no sign of moving, she stood undecided in her living room. Finally, with a sigh, she moved away from the bay windows.

What the hell am I doing? Alex thought, frustrated. *I'm back to stalking my ex. It would be laughable if it wasn't so damned pitiful. What am I so afraid of? Why don't I just go and say hello?*

She missed Megan. She missed being with her. And yet something stopped her from reaching out again, afraid of the rejection. Just as afraid if she wasn't rejected, because that would mean that she would need to be more forthcoming with her feelings, admit to her need.

Lost in turbulent thoughts, Alex failed to see the shadow approach until the tap on her window made her jump. She slowly rolled down the window…and fell into Megan's bottomless green eyes.

"So, were you going to just sit there for a while?"

"Yes. No." Alex shrugged, blushing.

Megan studied her. *She looks good.* She released a breath, annoyed that her pulse was racing. "So, which is it?"

"I'm thinking about it. Hanging out."

"I see. Okay." Megan turned to leave.

"Hey, Megan?" Alex called out. Megan threw her a questioning look over her shoulder. "You look good."

Megan had to shake her head at that. "So do you." Their eyes held an instant longer, then with a smile she left, feeling Alex's eyes on her back.

Still undecided, Alex hesitated as she watched Megan go back into the building. Then with a sigh, she got out and walked across to the front door. Her hand reached out to the doorbell a fraction of a second before the door swung open. Megan stared at her, lips parted as if surprised.

"I was just..."

"I was wondering..."

They had both spoken at the same time and with a nervous laugh, Megan stepped back inside. "You go."

Alex sighed. "I might have left a couple of boxes here when I moved out. I was wondering if it would be okay if I grabbed them now."

Something flickered in Megan's eyes, a momentary hurt that was quickly veiled. "Oh." She hid her disappointment behind a practical nod. "Sure. I haven't had time to rent out the place yet, so they're probably still sitting where you left them." The truth was, she hadn't wanted to rent the place, was unable to picture anyone else living there. She led the way through the store to the back entrance. Alex followed her wordlessly, searching for a way to break the silence. At the apartment door, Megan unlocked it and with a quick reach switched on the light just inside the entrance. She stepped back. "Here you go." She turned to leave. "Just close the door behind you when you are done."

Alex stared after her for a moment, longing, then turned in. Inside the empty apartment, she was assailed by memories. Like snapshots, memories of Megan, of their time together, crowded into her mind. She saw Megan as she had first seen her across this very doorway the day she moved in, eyes flashing as she shoved the lease at her. Each memory brought a sweet ache. She shook her head, determined not to revisit that part of her life. She had moved on. *Yeah, right,* the annoying little voice in her head answered. She ignored it. She had a case to worry about.

With quick, determined steps, she crossed to a small storage closet in the kitchen and found one forgotten box behind a garbage can. She pulled it out and sat on the kitchen floor as she dug into it. Her hand closed on soft cloth and pulled it out, her heart racing. She slowly unwound the fabric and stared at the police badge wrapped within. Dark rust spots speckled the shield, spots she knew were blood. She felt a tremor go through her as she looked at it. 5812. Sam's badge. Her trembling fingers touched the badge, and her heart felt as if a tight fist were squeezing it. *What does it all mean?* She was overwhelmed by what she was thinking, the possibilities she was faced with. *There has to be an explanation.*

Unable to stop the flood of emotion that rose up in her, she started to cry. She was shaken at the thought that something about Sam's death was starting to not ring true. Her mind was pulled to the alley once again, her brain remembering with vivid clarity the blood as it pooled between her fingers.

Megan stood in the doorway watching Alex. Part of her wanted to run to her, to put her arms around her. She stood help-lessly as she watched the sobs wrack the lean body, and she knew that she couldn't offer the comfort Alex needed. With one last helpless look, she left her sitting on the floor, crying as her own heart broke for the woman she still loved.

Lost in her turmoil, Alex never heard Megan's entrance or exit. She sat there for an hour, mired in confusion and grief. Her hands clutched the badge 'til the knuckles showed white. *Sam, what did you get yourself into?* she thought with a sense of disquiet. She stood up on trembling legs and shoved the badge into her pocket. She rubbed at her face, trying to erase the tears, trying at the same time to figure out what she needed to do next. She knew who she had to go see.

ALEX FOUND HERSELF parked outside of the dark brick building. She was nervous. Strange how that was the one feeling she could grasp onto. *What will I say? What can I say? Maybe I should call instead, or... Too late, there she is.* She stepped out of the car as the woman came out of headquarters; the sun against the glass in the structure was blinding.

Stacey didn't see her at first, too busy searching for her keys in her jacket pocket; but an awareness of being watched made her turn. Her eyes widened as she recognized Alex leaning against her car, and her steps faltered.

They hadn't seen each other since the investigation into the shooting of Chris Billings. Alex straightened up and waited for the stab of jealousy or the anger to flare. None came—only sadness and curiosity, in equal parts. "Stacey?"

Stacey nodded, her fingers nervously clenching by her side. "Hi, Alex."

Alex studied her. She was pale, shadows below her eyes. *There is pain there, grieving,* Alex thought with a start, and felt pity. She stayed with that feeling for a moment, puzzling over it. "Can we go somewhere to talk for a minute?"

Stacey's eyes flickered. Nerves. Her first instinct was to decline, but something in Alex's eyes stopped her. *Maybe we both need closure.* She led her across the street to a small coffee shop whose large bay windows advertised all-day breakfasts, and they settled in a booth, trying not to look at each other.

Alex sighed, knowing she would have to be the one to break the ice. "First off, I know all about you and Sam. She told me about you."

Stacey paled; the hands that had been nervously toying with a spoon stopped. "I'm so very sorry. You must hate me."

Alex looked at her, seeing in the deep brown eyes and sharp features what Sam had been attracted to. It should have bothered her, and she was surprised it didn't. *Am I finally over it? Over Sam?* "I don't hate you. I really don't have anything against you. I just disagreed with what you did... what you both did. But in all honesty, I have to take some of the blame for the relationship being messed up enough that an affair was easy for her."

"Never easy. She still loved you."

Alex nodded. She had known that too. Alex was amazed at the compassion she felt toward the woman who had been part of her betrayal. Where was the anger? The hurt? Buried with Sam, she supposed. She no longer had the energy to be angry; it was time to release Stacey from the guilt she so obviously felt.

"Stacey, we had stopped being in love long before you came along. We should have ended then, but years of being with someone can be as powerful a tie as love. Though it becomes destructive over time." Alex was amazed at how calm she felt.

Stacey didn't say anything, but in her eyes there was gratitude, a quiet acknowledgment of the gift that Alex was offering her. They stared at each other, trying to understand the rules of behavior for a situation like theirs—strangers, yet connected in a very intimate way.

Alex felt something squeeze her heart then let go. "You really loved her, didn't you?"

Pain crossed Stacey's face. "Yeah." She looked out of the window. They sat quietly for a few minutes, each lost in thought. It was new territory for the both of them.

A waitress with lanky brown hair stopped by to take their order. Her gum smacked as they ordered coffee. She pushed her note pad into the front pocket of her apron and, with dangling silver bangles jingling on her wrist, poured them a cup of coffee and threw a few creamers onto the table.

The silence lengthened as they each prepared their coffee. After stirring hers for a moment, Alex carefully placed her spoon on a paper napkin and looked at Stacey. "Listen, I need to ask you something about the investigation into that night."

She didn't have to say which night it was; Stacey's eyes narrowed. "I can't talk to you about the investigation."

"You cleared me, remember?"

Stacey looked away. "I know, but I still can't talk to you about the investigation. I'm sorry."

Alex nodded. "What if I ask some questions, could you answer them?"

The brunette sighed. "Alex..."

"It might be important."

Stacey hesitated. Her eyes stayed on Alex's face as she debated. The investigation was still a sore spot. She had gone against everything that she had believed in, everything she stood for, by ending it almost before it had begun. But something in Alex's eyes had her releasing a long breath. "What do you want to know?"

"The man who shot her, the man I killed... Chris Billing, was it?"

"Yeah."

"Did you find anything peculiar in his past? Any connection to the Bayview?"

Stacey studied Alex as she thought about the question. Her shrug was slight. "Not much. Small time stuff—dealing drugs, that sort of thing. I do remember that his last known place of residence was the Bayview. Why?"

"I'm working on a murder case at the Bayview. Someone named Monica Webb." Alex rubbed the back of her neck. She was so far from finding the answer, and yet she couldn't shake the feeling that it was right in front of her. Whatever it was. "Do you have any idea if he would have known Sam?"

There was a slight hesitation. "Sam? No. Where did you get that?"

"I didn't. I just..." She shrugged. "Do you know if Sam ever stayed at the Bayview?"

"That dump? Are you kidding? What's going on? Why all the questions about Sam?"

Alex rubbed at her eyes. "I've never been big on coincidences. I just keep sensing that there is a connection between my case and Sam's death. I know it sounds farfetched. Sam's death appeared to be a random shooting by some doped-up loser. But suddenly this loser's name shows up in another murder location, in a hotel registry right alongside Sam's... I mean, what the hell would she be doing at the Bayview, the same place as this Billings character who shot her?" She suddenly looked embarrassed. "The only thing I could come up with... I thought maybe that was where..."

Stacey's eyes widened. "You thought we might have used the Bayview?"

Alex shrugged. "Well, hell, I'm sorry if that is insulting, but you will forgive me for not knowing the full details of your...what should we call it? Relationship?"

There is leftover anger after all, she thought with a start. She waved her hand in a half apology. "Forget it. That's not what I wanted to talk to you about."

Stacey's eyes were sad. "Alex, I'm sorry if this is really screwed up. I don't blame you for being angry. I can't even lie to you and say I didn't know she was with you, because obviously I did—from when I dated Darcy. It, whatever it was, just happened; and it was a shitty thing to do. But no, we were never at the Bayview."

Alex nodded. "So, what would she be doing checking into the Bayview? Something feels odd to me. I don't know..." She didn't mention the third coincidence that clinched it for her: Sam's badge number showing up on four separate arrests sheets as Billings' arresting officer. Not yet.

She watched a couple in the next booth having a heated argument. Her eyes returned to Stacey. "Stacey, did Sam ever talk about work—a case she was working on, anything?"

Stacey pushed a slow breath out of her mouth. "Not really. We tried not to. In the last few months of the affair, she was upset and distracted. She kept disappearing, or else not showing up after we had made plans to meet." She shrugged. "I thought it had to do with you and the guilt she was feeling." There was a long pause before she continued. "I know that she was really upset about something a few weeks before her death."

There was silence as they each absorbed what the words really meant. Stacey was still talking to Sam a few weeks before her death. Alex frowned and waited for the flare of anger. None came. Only a sudden wave of sadness and tremendous tiredness. *All the lies, and for what? To avoid making the tough choices? What an absolute waste.*

"I'm sorry," Stacey said, as if reading her mind.

Alex nodded, unable to drum up any anger. "Did she say what she was upset about?"

Stacey stared into the distance, trying to recall the conversation. It was an area she rarely ventured into. The pain was there, below the surface, like an ache that crops up every change of weather. "She had stumbled on something that pointed to a cop being dirty, but she didn't say who or what. Just that she was going to confront whoever it was. I guess she never got the chance."

Chapter
Twenty-One

JAMIE SLUMPED IN the passenger seat and stared out of the window at the passing traffic. She didn't know why, but she felt put out. She crossed her arms and tried to ignore the fact that she was almost pouting. "Tell me again why we have to meet someone from the DA's office?"

"Because she says she has some information for us," Alex answered in the overtly patient tone that a parent takes after being asked the same question more than once.

"Why is she involved at all? I have enough people from the district attorney's office breathing down my neck without having to invite one more in," Jamie grumbled.

"Jamie, she may have information about Sam that ties the two cases together."

Jamie turned to look at her. "I still don't get how you got from Sam's murder, months ago, to the random killing of a hooker in some dive. Sam was killed by a drug dealer. The fact that the name of this drug dealer showed up in the registration book of the same fleabag hotel as our murder is hardly surprising. I bet if you checked, his name would appear all over the city in countless other dumps. That's hardly earth-shattering news. The so-called evidence is way too flimsy to hang this investigation on."

Alex sighed. She knew that Jamie thought she was on a wild goose chase fueled by the guilt she felt about Sam, and maybe she was right. Still, she needed to see it to the end. Instinct told her she was on the right path. She had learned over the years to listen to the little voice in her head, even when it was annoying.

"Jamie, maybe I am totally off base and the two things are not related. I admit that it could be possible for the same guy to show up in two separate places where a murder is taking place. But you have to agree that Sam's name appearing on the register at some dive in the middle of all of this around the time that he was also there, tells me that I have to at least look at the possibility that they are related. I'm not big on coincidence. Finding out she was Billings' arresting officer on four separate occasions—who, by the way, ends up with his gun shoved against her head—tells me I've got to look at the whole picture." She turned a corner. "And if you weren't so pissed that you weren't the one who figured all of this out, you would agree with me. I told you what Stacey told me when I first met with her—Sam was chasing after a cop that had turned."

Jamie's teeth worried her lower lip and she shook her head. She was afraid of what they might discover. Instinct told her that whatever had died with Sam was about to come out once again, and the answers might not be something they wanted to hear. She had hoped that it would stay buried with Sam; now she only hoped they would be strong enough to survive finding the truth, whatever it was. "You going to take her word? What does she know?"

Despite Jamie's misgivings, Alex knew she couldn't stop pursuing it, though she couldn't say what was driving her. Alex frowned. "You don't have to come along, you know."

"I'm here now, aren't I?"

Alex almost smiled. They really were almost like an old married couple—grumbling and bitching their way through the day. "Well, if I'm wrong, you can say 'I told you so' for as long as you like." She pulled up and parked the car in front of a decrepit building that might have been imposing a long time before. After turning off the engine, she turned to the blonde beside her. "Are you coming? Or are you going to stay here moping 'cause you are not quite in control of your case?"

Because that hit too close to home, Jamie snorted as she swung the door open. "Give me a break. Let's go." She stared at the faded sign, the boarded-up windows on the second floor, the peeling plaster...and shuddered. "Model Café? For crying out loud..."

They pushed open the torn screen door and stopped in the entrance, assaulted as soon as they entered by the smell of cigarette smoke, old beer, and countless other odors it was best not to try and figure out. Their feet immediately stuck to the floor, and Alex tried not to think about what kind of substances were spilt on the worn wooden floor. Her eyes stung as they narrowed against the thick smoke that hung above them, seemingly a permanent fixture.

Directly in front of them, the regulars were glued to wobbly stools that wrapped around a large oak bar that might—at some time—have looked impressive. Some watched, with one eye, whatever sport was playing on the old television set nailed above them in the corner of the bar. The set had colors that were washed out and the picture was blurry, but it didn't seem to matter. On the left, a pool table took up most of the space, and four men nursing their beers paused their game to watch the new arrivals with interest.

Alex squinted and tried to see through the thick, blue haze. She saw no sign of Stacey, so she made her way to one of the cracked red leather booths on the right. Jamie followed.

They sat down, and Jamie made a face as she looked around. "Hard to believe that this was a hot spot when I was in college."

Alex grinned. "They were the only ones who didn't ask for ID."

Her eyes caught a new arrival at the door. The pool players paused again. Stacey stood uncertainly as she hesitated at the entrance looking for them. When she saw Alex, a look of relief crossed her face and she made her way to them, ignoring the drunken leers as she passed by the bar. She gingerly sat on the opposite side of the booth, and avoided putting her hands anywhere near the sticky table top. "Hi."

"Stacey, you remember Jamie?"

Jamie's nod was curt. "You hang out at the nicest places," she tossed out.

Stacey shrugged. "It's where she hangs out."

Alex leaned forward. "Who does? What is this about?"

Stacey pushed a nervous hand through her thick brown hair. "Before I start, I just want...I would..." She sighed. "Look, I don't want my name connected in any way with whatever comes out of your investigation."

"If that is how you feel, why get involved at all?" Jamie waved a hand. "Why this?"

Stacey hesitated, her eyes shadowed. "I felt I owed it to Sam to check things out. I owed it to Alex to share what I found out. The rest is up to you."

Jamie snorted, then shrugged when Alex threw her an impatient look.

If Stacey noticed, she gave no sign of it. She glanced at Alex. "After we met, a name stuck in my mind, something familiar. Monica Webb."

"The hooker?" asked Alex.

"Yeah. So I went back and took a look at the files and the notes from the investigation into Sam's shooting and her killer's shooting." There was a quick, cautious look toward Alex, then she continued. "I discovered a few things that tweaked my interest. This Webb character was Billings' so-called steady."

"His girlfriend?"

"So to speak." She shrugged. "I also took a look at the autopsy report." She shuddered at the memory. She had avoided looking at it for the duration of the investigation. A couple of nights previously, after fortifying herself with tequila, she had snuck into the records room and looked at it. As she looked at the glossy pictures and read the notes, she had broken down inside the dusty, crowded room, grateful that no one was around to see her lose it behind the beat-up filing cabinets. She took a deep breath. "Sam was not shot by Billings' gun."

"What?" they roared in unison. Alex almost jumped off the bench.

"The bullet entered from the right; and if your recollection of the event is correct, Billings couldn't have shot her, as he was standing to the left. The bullet fragment that was found was also the wrong caliber. It was a .38, and Billings had a .45.

Stunned by the words, Alex sat digesting the news. Of all the things she had expected, that was not one of them.

Jamie was furious. "Why the hell is this coming out now? Why didn't it come out during your investigation?"

Stacey sighed and rubbed at her eyes. "Because I ended the investigation into her death."

"You what?" she growled. A few heads turned in their direction at the commotion, the attention quickly fading as most of them returned to their own misery.

"I didn't want Alex to go through a prolonged trial."

Jamie stared at her, suddenly suspicious. "You mean *you* didn't want go through it." Stacey lifted her eyes to meet Jamie's accusing look.

Lost in thought, Alex watched the interplay, trying to grasp what it all meant, trying to make sense of it all. Where were they now with their case? She tried to remember that night, the irony not lost on her that up until this point she had tried so hard to forget everything about it. Now she tried to remember more than just Billings turning and the sound of the gun going off and the vision of Sam crumpling to the pavement. *What did I miss? How could there have been more than what I saw?* She was unable to remember any other details.

Stacey was momentarily taken aback by Jamie's aggressive tone. She sighed, defeated. "Okay, *I* didn't want to. I was a mess and I didn't think I could go through it. And I didn't think Alex could or should. I didn't want Alex to find out about Sam and me if I could help it. I didn't want that to be her last memory."

"I already knew about it." Alex's quiet tone broke into the increasingly volatile tension. She glanced at Jamie, then at Stacey. "I don't think I could have gone through a long trial, so I guess I have to thank you for that. Except now I have more questions than answers. If Billings didn't shoot her, then who the hell did?" They exchanged long looks.

"I'm sorry." There was a pause. "I found one more thing. It could be nothing." Stacey shrugged. "The Webb woman had a roommate at the time—Christie Bell, a dancer."

Jamie sat back in frustration. She hadn't turned up any room-mate in her investigation. She hadn't found the connection to Bill-ings. What more was she missing? *Who the hell is running this investigation, anyway?* She felt the frustration build. More than peeved that she was dropping the ball all over the place, she glared at Stacey, who pretended not to see it.

Stacey looked around. "She sort of disappeared for a while, but I think I found her. She usually works here."

Alex stared at her, absorbed the news, then nodded. "Wait here." They watched her make her way to the bar and motion to the heavy-set man who stood leaning against the bar, watching the game. She chatted with him for a second or two and returned hold-ing three glasses of whatever was on tap. She plopped herself down. "She hasn't been around the last couple of nights. He said to try Wally's."

Stacey stood up. "I'm sorry I can't do more. I hope it helps." She hesitated, wanting to say more but unable to find the words. With one last look, she left quickly, not turning back.

Jamie stared at her retreating back. "Well, if that doesn't beat everything." She shook her head. "I don't know whether or not to believe her."

"I do."

"You do? You trust her?"

Alex stood up. "Yes."

Jamie followed suit. "Why?"

"Because she loved Sam more than I did."

SHE WASN'T AT Wally's, but one of the dancers there pointed them to another joint. At the fourth one, their patience had run out and they both felt frayed around the edges. Jamie got out of the car and slammed the door with a bit more force than was necessary. "I wish someone had warned me I was going to dive-hop today; I would have worn other clothes."

Exasperated, Alex turned to her. "Jamie, how long has it been since you've had sex?"

"What the hell does that have to do with anything?"

"I'm trying to figure out why you're so cranky. Either you need to get laid, or else it's early onset of menopause."

Jamie opened her mouth to blast Alex back, but she couldn't think of a clever enough comeback and nothing came out. Her mouth closed with a snap. "Shut up." It was the best she could manage under the circumstances.

Alex just shook her head as she pushed the door open, paused in the doorway, and let her eyes adjust to the dim light. After a quick glance around the room, she crossed to the bar and with a head motion called the bartender over. She watched him take his time, her mouth tightening with rising frustration. She had lost her sense of humor somewhere between the first bar and the last. All the holes were starting to look the same, including the bartenders. Her clothes smelled like the inside of an ashtray, and her eyes felt gritty from too much smoke. Her head was too full of questions and not enough answers, and more than anything she wanted to sit somewhere quiet to think it all through. "Hey, is Christie around?"

"Who wants to know?" He was thick around the middle and the neck, his biceps impressive as he wiped the bar.

"A friend."

His pale eyes fixed on her. She pushed a wrinkled twenty-dollar bill toward him and his eyes flickered to it and away. With a quick glance around, his big paw swallowed the bill so quickly that Alex raised an impressed eyebrow. "She might be."

He pulled a dirty rag from his shoulder and started to wipe a glass. Alex made a silent vow never to order anything that required a glass at any bar again. She slipped another twenty on the bar. As his large hand closed on it, she grabbed his wrist with surprising strength. She kept her tone pleasant, but there was no mistaking the steely warning.

"I'll only play for so long." He licked his fleshy lips, suddenly nervous; then he made a show of nonchalance as he shrugged. She held his wrist a fraction longer, then relaxed her hold. "So, where can I find her?"

"You a cop?"

"Does it matter?"

He hesitated briefly then motioned with his head toward the back. "She's in there, getting ready. The dark-haired one." His scooped the twenty and resumed his wiping.

Alex straightened and with a quick motion to Jamie started to cross to the back. Jamie followed, eyebrows raised in question. "She's over there somewhere."

As they passed through the narrow back hallway, assailed by the stench of urine and unwashed bodies, they paused to let their eyes adjust to the dimmer light. A bare light bulb hung from the ceiling on a black electrical cord, and the weak light was barely enough to enable them to see the doors. One was marked private. Jamie looked at her. "Are you the good cop or the bad cop this time?"

Alex grinned. "I have no idea. Let's play it by ear."

She gave a quick rap, then tried the door without waiting for an answer. It was unlocked. She pushed the door wider and they

both entered. Unlike the dim hallway, this room was lit with fluo-
rescent lighting. They blinked as they adjusted to the brightness.
Once a storage room, it had been converted into a poor version of a
dressing room. A narrow table bolted in front of a blurry mirror
took up most of the room. The table was filled with assorted jars
and tubes of make-up and powder. A lopsided coat rack stood to
the side, and from it hung various undergarments and pieces of
clothing. The room was filled with a layer of cigarette smoke and
heavy sweet perfume, and something else that smelled vaguely
familiar.

A dark-haired woman watched them enter and her face tightened, her eyes growing suspicious. Even from a distance, her body
language wasn't hard to read.

Alex tried to keep her face friendly. "Christie?"

The brunette who had been watching from the corner
shrugged, took a deep drag from her cigarette and blew the smoke
in their direction. "Who wants to know?"

Jamie did a slow burn at the arrogance. She pulled a wooden
chair over and sat down. "A friend of a friend."

The brunette flicked ashes onto the floor and crossed to the
table. With careless disregard—or perhaps to get a reaction—she
dropped her ratty bathrobe and stood naked in front of the mirror.
She grabbed a make-up brush and started to apply a coat of powder
to her cheekbones. "I've got a lot of friends."

Alex scanned the naked body in front of her. The woman was
anywhere between thirty and forty, the face under the thick make-
up appearing younger than her attitude. Her body was reasonably
fit, though her breasts were obviously not what nature had pro-
vided. Alex's eyes caught Jamie's bored look, and she almost
smiled. They had never been into dancers. She lifted her eyes back
to the performer, who was watching her in the mirror, lips curled.
"Monica Webb ring any bells?"

"Nope." But she hadn't been quick enough to hide the flicker
of recognition on her face.

"You sure, now?"

The dancer stepped closer to Alex, a little too close for comfort.
For a moment Alex was taken aback, not quite knowing where to
look—trying to avoid looking at the full breasts swinging so close
in her direction, and not being able to look down, either. She
stopped herself from stepping back, kept a bored look on her face,
let her eyes drift over the body, then met the waiting blue eyes of
the brunette who was watching her with calculated coolness.

"Like what you see, detective?" She had made them for cops
the minute they had walked in.

So, she isn't as stupid as she pretends. Alex sighed, tired of the night. Maybe Jamie's crankiness had rubbed off on her; she wasn't in the mood to play. "Christie, we can do this all night if you want. Which means you'll miss your number, which means lost tips. Or you can put that robe back on and answer our questions, and we'll be out of here before the license on those tits expires."

Jamie swallowed a laugh. The woman's mouth tightened, and for a brief moment Jamie thought she was going to use those fake red nails to scratch Alex's face. She tensed, ready to jump in if needed.

Instead the woman surprised her by starting to laugh. The laugh was softer and more youthful than expected. She stooped and caught her robe and stepped into it. She glanced at them, somehow amused. "Want a drink?" she asked as she crossed back to the crowded table.

"No thanks. So, about Monica Webb?"

She paused in her pouring. "What about her?"

"We understand you girls were roommates once?"

Monica leaned a hip against the side of the wobbly table. "Yeah. A hundred years ago, before she started to turn tricks. I dance, but I don't go for that shit, you know?"

The detectives exchanged glances. "Did you know the guy she dated last year?"

"She dated hundreds of guys."

"Billings?"

For a moment the aloof mask slipped and a look of hatred crossed her face. It was seconds only, and if they hadn't been studying her so closely they would have missed it.

"Yeah, I know him." She spat out the words and turned away. "Listen, if that's all, I have to get ready."

"Christie, I was the one that shot and killed him...after he killed my girlfriend," Alex told her, gambling on her reaction.

Christie turned. "For real?"

"For real."

The mask slipped further and she sat down. She studied Alex for a moment. "He was a down-and-out prick. He got his kicks hitting girls, you know. Monica—she wanted no part of him, but she was afraid to call it quits. He pushed her around a bit. I'm glad he's dead." For a moment the hardness was back.

"Was he her pimp?" Jamie asked.

She turned her attention to Jamie. "Pimp? Him? Nah. He was more into breaking things—like bones. Then he got in with some cop downtown. I think he was going around doing the dirty work for a cut of the drug profits. He started walking around like he was a big shot. Monica—she found out and was spooked. She started writing things down in her diary. She thought drugs was bad news."

Jamie and Alex exchanged a look. "Do you know where that diary is now?" Jamie asked casually.

She shrugged. "No. She used to just have it lying around, but who knows?"

Alex fought to keep her tone indifferent. "The cop, do you have any idea who he was?"

Monica looked at Alex, then at Jamie. "It wasn't a he, it was a she."

"SERGEANT KANE?"

The uniformed officer tipped down the newspaper he was reading. When he saw Alex standing on the opposite side of his desk, he shot to his feet. He had been a below-average beat cop, prone to cutting too many corners and taking the easy way out. In the ten years he had spent on the street, he had never had the stomach to make the tough arrests, the difficult choices one had to make. He had always been more suited to the life of a desk jockey. He had discovered his true calling as the person in charge of the evidence room. He was known around the station as meticulous in his paperwork and anal about the details on his reports. Alex was counting on that.

"Hey, Detective. I have that printout you requested right here."

The evidence warehouse was Sergeant Kane's domain. Alex had called ahead with her request, which the sergeant was flattered to grant. "You didn't give me much notice, but it was only a matter of pulling up the records from one year ago and printing them out."

Alex scanned the sheets, hoping a name would jump out at her... and equally afraid that it would. "Is it within the realm of possibility—not probable, just possible—that an officer could...borrow a weapon from the warehouse without your knowledge?"

"No." He was insulted and he looked it, his fleshy jowls turning pink.

She could almost see his chest puffing out, his extra pounds bouncing over his belt and stretching his uniform shirt. "It's not possible?"

He frowned at her. "I keep strict records, Detective."

"Yes, I see." She scanned the printout one more time. "It's just that it appears that a whole month is missing. The month of June..."

"What? That's impossible." He grabbed the pages from her hand, his face turning purple in outrage. His small, pale eyes searched the printout. He lifted his head and slapped the sheets

down on the desk. "Someone ripped the month off this printout."
He shifted back on the balls of his feet.

"Who would do that?" He stepped back, blinking rapidly. A
bead of sweat appeared on his forehead, and Alex stared at its
progress down his face in sudden fascination. "Sergeant?"

He cleared his throat, looking quickly left, then right. "I
dunno."

She nodded once, pursing her lips. "Okay. Thanks for your
time, Sergeant." She turned to leave, then stopped at the doorway
as if a sudden thought had just occurred to her. "Oh...Sergeant, do
you back your hard drive up on a regular basis?"

Annoyed that his formerly unimpeachable reputation was
compromised, he nodded without thinking. "Of course. Every
month."

Alex stepped closer to the desk. "Can I see the original for
June?"

Chapter
Twenty-Two

JAMIE LED KATE down the narrow hallway of police head-quarters to the detectives' room. She wanted Kate to look at some mug shots in search of a blond Sam Spade, hoping that looking at pictures would jar her memory concerning the man she had seen that night at the Bayview. It was a very long shot.

"Wait here," Jamie instructed, pulling out a chair for Kate. The witness sat slowly, her eyes taking in everything. "Don't touch anything. I need to go get Alex."

Jamie was worried about her partner, who was obsessing about the case. She was on some sort of crusade, and she was scary in her focused determination. Several hours earlier, Alex had left the bar without another word, and her frustration had shimmered from her in waves. She had slammed the car door and, after starting the car, had pulled away, giving Jamie barely enough time to get in.

One look at her face and Jamie knew to stay quiet. They had not discussed Sam's shooting or the stunning news delivered by Stacey. Then Alex had disappeared for a few hours, and she had no idea where she had gone; but Jamie was afraid to bring it up.

Jamie couldn't help but feel that their investigation was in dis-array. They were chasing a vapor trail. The instant they thought they were making headway, a new discovery turned everything upside down. The news was disturbing all around. Jamie couldn't help but feel that they had opened the proverbial Pandora's box, and they were not going to like what they found inside.

She went in search of Alex and found her sorting out binders filled with pictures. "She's here."

Alex looked at her, noticed the strain on her face. "You okay?"

"Nothing I can't handle. You?"

"Same."

"Well, here is a sight for sore eyes." Andrew stood looming in the doorway.

Alex didn't look up from her search. "Go away, we're busy."

"Is that your witness?" Andrew nodded slightly toward the other room.

"Yeah."

"Not exactly a tough assignment, eh, girls?" He grinned. "Let me know if you need a man to take care of that one."

Alex made a face. "Pig. What are you doing here anyway?"

"Paperwork hell. Trying to catch up." He left the two of them selecting the mug books they wanted to use and returned to Jamie's office.

"Hi there, ma'am, can I get you a cup of coffee while you wait?"

Kate spun around in the comfortable swivel chair and faced a nice-looking man who wore a suit and a friendly grin. "No thanks," she said, instinctively answering his smile. "I'm fine."

Andrew didn't leave, but leaned up against the edge of Jamie's cubicle and made himself comfortable. "I understand you've had a rough week," he said in a soothing voice.

Must be another cop thing, Kate thought before answering. "Yeah, you could say that."

His smile showed genuine concern. "Are you handling it all right? It's not easy to have your whole world turned upside down, I know." He offered his hand. "My name is Andrew Rhodes. I'm a good friend of Alex's." He didn't relinquish her hand right away. "If anyone can solve this case, she can."

"I'm sure you're right." She looked down at her hand, amused. He grinned at the unspoken message and reluctantly released it. "Have you known her a long time?"

"Yeah, ages. We went to school together. Jamie, too. I taught them all they know." He grinned.

She had to smile again. The boyish grin was harmless. They chatted on for a while about school and break-ins.

Andrew shifted, moving his weight from one foot to the other. "Maybe when this mess is all over, I can give you a call? There's a great Thai place downtown."

My God, is he asking me out on a date? Kate would have laughed if she hadn't been afraid of offending him. "But I don't think—"

"Don't turn me down now," he interrupted, "It's just a thought, that's all."

Alex saved her, appearing behind Andrew. "What's a thought?"

"I just asked Kate if she'd like to have dinner with me some-time."

Alex pushed Andrew away. "Hitting on the witnesses is con-sidered bad form. Go away, Andrew."

As he turned, Kate stared at him, puzzled. He suddenly looked familiar. Something in the shape of head, his profile. She had seen him before...but where?

Alex watched Kate watch him, reading the recognition in her eyes, and for some reason, she slowly felt the hair at the base of her neck rise. She frowned suddenly, trying to quiet her unease. "Hey, Andrew?" He turned to her. "Ever stayed at the Bayview?"

Andrew turned slowly. There was a brief tightening of his jaw, but then he laughed. To Alex, it sounded forced. "That dump? Yeah, all the time," he joked. "Why?"

Alex shrugged, faking nonchalance. "No reason." She glanced at her email, and the one from Sergeant Kane caught her attention. He had found the microfiche and had sent her the missing page. As she casually rolled through the list of names of officers who had signed off weapons for the month of June, one made her eyes flicker as her heart dropped. She turned to glance at Kate, who was staring at her in confusion. "I changed my mind about looking at the books. We've got to go."

"But what about the photos..." She stopped as Alex all but pulled her out of the chair.

"Never mind that. Maybe later." Alex's eyes searched for Jamie, who had stopped to chat with Andrew. "James? I gotta go. I'll call you."

"What? What do you mean you have to..." She didn't get a response as Alex disappeared around the corner. She threw a puzzled look toward Andrew. "Well, that was weird."

He watched them leave, thoughtful. "Yeah, since Sam's death..."

ON THEIR WAY back to Kate's, the two women did not exchange a word. One look at Alex's face had warned Kate to stay silent. Something was wrong. "Tomorrow you're packing and getting out of here for a while," Alex finally said.

"No."

Alex continued as if she hadn't heard her. "You're going somewhere I know you will be safe."

"No." Kate turned her head, suddenly frustrated at not being able to have a say in her life. "No. I am not going to run away like a child. Not unless you tell me what the hell is going on." As Alex opened her mouth to protest, Kate raised a hand in warning. "I deserve that much. You tell me exactly what happened back there. I've had enough. All of a sudden I have cops living in my house; I'm told when to come and go; I can't even take a bath in privacy, for God's sake! And if I want to kiss a woman, there is nothing you or your detective pal can do about it."

Alex managed to stop just short of laughing out loud, but Kate noticed her amusement and felt the frustration at the loss of control in her life rise to the surface. She barely waited for the car to come to a stop before jumping out. "Put a patrol car in the driveway, if you want, but I don't want anyone in my house tonight."

Alex raced after her. "Kate, wait."

"No."

Alex placed a hand on her arm. "Be reasonable."

Kate shook free. "Reasonable? I've been nothing but reasonable. I want my damn life back. You guys have nothing. And if someone wants to harm me, well—I'll take my chances."

One look at her determined face and Alex knew there was nothing she could do to persuade her. She hesitated, then nodded. "I'll post an extra car in front. Kate, please call me if you see anything that makes you nervous. Anything. You know I'll be here in a flash."

Kate's look softened. "I know, Alex." She gently touched her cheek. "I hope Megan realizes what she's got."

Alex looked at her for a moment, then with a slight smile she left, lost in thought.

THE CAR WAS again parked in the same spot. Megan paced away from the window. She was confused about what to do, part of her wanting to go and ask her in, part of her—the part still hurting—wanting to ignore her. With a quiet sigh, she grabbed her jacket and went out.

Alex saw her come out of the front door, and this time rolled down her window as Megan crossed the street to her.

"Evening, officer."

"Evening."

"Just hanging out?"

"Yeah."

"They have laws against that sort of thing, you know."

Alex shrugged and grinned. "Where is a cop when you need one?"

"Where indeed? Going to be hanging out for long?"

"Not long."

Megan smiled. "Okay then, I'll leave you to it."

"Okay."

"Still drinking your coffee black?"

"Yes."

"Good to know. Good night."

"Night."

Alex followed her progress across the street. It had been an impulse—showing up there. After dropping Kate off and driving around for an hour, she had started to feel claustrophobic. She had even started to feel scared, terrified that she was standing on the edge of some abyss. Too many questions were unanswered, and the answers she was finding were frightening in their implications.

Sam had been involved in something. She was now certain of it. She was beginning to suspect that maybe Andrew knew something about it. The microfiche had shown that Andrew had signed out a gun two days before Sam's death, and the gun was never recovered. The gun had been the same caliber as the murder weapon. Coincidence again? It was a common caliber. And it could mean anything. That gun might have been evidence he needed for a case.

Overwhelmed by her swirling thoughts, she sat in front of Megan's house feeling paranoid. *What if I'm right? What if Sam's accident was not a random shooting?* Her eyes caught the light that switched on in Megan's front window. On impulse, she got out of the car and quickly crossed the road.

"I'm sorry. I didn't know where else to go," she said as Megan opened the door.

Megan gave her a long, quiet look. She recognized the haunted look in Alex's eyes, the whiteness around her mouth, the exhaustion that lay heavy across her shoulders. Without another word, she opened the door wider to let her in. "Want a drink?" she offered.

"Okay." Alex sat down on the sofa and stared at her hands, lost in thought. She flinched when Megan touched her on the shoulder, then smiled faintly as she accepted the glass of wine. Now that she was there, she didn't know what she wanted to say.

Sensing her mood, Megan sat beside her and took a sip of wine. After a moment, she looked at her unexpected visitor and asked, "What's got you so twisted, Alex?"

Alex shook her head. "I can't..." She saw Megan's face reflect her hurt, and quickly placed her glass on the side table. "I can't begin to know where to start."

Megan took a slow breath and quietly released it. "Start at the beginning."

Needing to pace, Alex stood up. "I'm not sure I even know where the beginning is. I am involved in a case that at first appeared to be routine." She gave a short laugh. "Routine for a murder, in any event." She shoved a hand through her hair. "But now it's no longer routine, and it is possibly tied to Sam's death, and it could be that Sam was in fact involved in some illegal stuff. And that her murder was premeditated, not an accident." She stopped pacing. "Or maybe...just maybe, I am losing my mind."

She looked so lost and in turmoil that Megan's heart went out to her. She stood up.

"I haven't slept in three days," Alex continued. "And my mind is going crazy trying to piece everything together." She took a trembling breath. "I just want it to stop." Her hand scrubbed at her face. "Sorry, Megan. I should go. I'm really not very good company." She turned to leave. "You and I can talk when I make more sense."

"Wait." Megan's quiet word stopped her at the door. "Stay. We don't have to talk or anything." She reached out her hand and Alex took it. Megan pulled her back. "I was just making some soup. When was the last time you ate?" Alex frowned, trying to remember. Megan shook her head. "Never mind. Come on." She stepped into the kitchen and turned the stove on to heat the pot already sitting there. She motioned toward a cutting board. "You can slice some bread."

Alex took the thick loaf and found the bread knife from memory. She sliced the bread, all the while trying to figure out a way of breaking the quiet. She felt lost, unable to find the right words. They continued preparing the meal in silence. Megan warmed two bowls and placed them on the breakfast bar. Once the soup was poured they sat down, and Alex suddenly realized that she was starving. She sampled the broth. "This is good. What's in it?"

Megan smiled. "Vegetables."

Alex had another spoonful. "No, really, what's in it?"

Megan looked at her, amused. "Vegetables. You know—like potatoes, carrots...all the stuff that's good for you."

"This doesn't look like vegetables. Where are the chunks?"

Megan shook her head. "It's pureed."

Feeling foolish, Alex looked down at her bowl. "Oh...well, it's good."

Megan watched her with a smile. *She is just too cute.*

After dinner they went back to the living room, and Alex hesitated in the middle of the room. "Thanks for the soup. I should be going."

"Where?"

"Where what?"

"Where are you going?"

Alex shrugged. "I don't know. Back to Jamie's, I guess."

Megan gave her a level look. "You don't have to go."

"What?"

She blushed. "I mean, I was going to just watch television. You can stay for a bit, keep the demons at bay a while longer," she added, understanding what Alex was most afraid of.

They settled on the couch, and to Alex it was as close to peace as she had felt since leaving Megan months before. She settled her head against the leather couch and sighed. Megan stretched her legs out beside her and turned the set on. They watched without really noticing the program that was on. Neither could concentrate on the story, so they just let the flickering images and the noise fill the space, content merely to be there together. At least for the moment, that was enough.

Megan felt Alex looking at her and turned her head. Their eyes met and she felt the heat straight through to her heart.

"I never ever meant to hurt you, Megan."

"I know."

"After Sam died, I swore I would never let anyone close again." Alex stared at her hands and felt Megan shift beside her. She lifted her head and stared at her.

Megan felt the look almost as a physical touch. Her skin heated everywhere and she felt out of breath. She swallowed and forced herself to look away, suddenly wanting distance. She focused on the conversation instead. "That's understandable. I just wish you had told me about her and about what happened. That is what hurt. For us to be so close and for you to say nothing. I kept hoping that you would. And to find out from someone else that you had gone back to work...it made me feel unimportant."

"God, Megan, you were never that. Maybe you were too important, and I didn't know how to handle that. I wish I had told you. I never could find the right words." She sighed. "I always felt like I had failed Sam in more ways than that one." At Megan's look of inquiry, she continued. "She had an affair while we were together, and I wondered if it was because she knew I didn't love her enough. Then I met you, and suddenly it became so clear that what Sam and I had didn't come close to what I was feeling for you. And she was dead, and I was able to go on and get that chance at love, and it made me feel so guilty."

Megan touched her hand and Alex's fingers curled to gently hold it, her thumb caressing Megan's index knuckle. "Megan, this case I'm involved in, it won't end well. I can sense it. But I can't stop. I have to get to the bottom of it because it involves Sam, and I owe her that. My head feels like it's about to blow off with all of the questions that I have, but I think I'm getting close to finding the answers. But not once have you not been in my thoughts too. I am hoping that when it is done, you and I can talk. I've missed you."

Megan felt the pull of the softly spoken words, and her eyes closed briefly. "Okay." Alex lifted her hand and gently kissed her palm. The tenderness of that brought an ache to Megan's heart that made her sigh. Her free hand briefly stroked the dark head. After exchanging looks, they turned their attention back to the television.

Into the second hour, Megan saw that Alex was falling asleep.

She shifted slightly, and without a word, put her arm around Alex. With a soft sigh, more asleep than awake, Alex settled into her, resting her head against Megan's neck. The natural movement made her smile. She felt the heat from Alex's body next to hers and toyed with the idea of waking her. *I really missed this, missed her.* Alex mumbled something. Unable to stop herself, Megan kissed the top of her head. "What is it, honey?"

"I miss you," Alex whispered as sleep overtook her.

Waking a few hours later, feeling more refreshed than she had in weeks, Alex pulled herself gently from Megan's hold. She waited, staring down at her, but Megan didn't wake. With a quiet smile, Alex pulled a blanket from the back of the sofa and covered Megan. Acting on impulse, she kissed her. "Thanks."

Back in the car, she glanced at her watch; it was ten o'clock. The unease returned. She felt unsettled and she wasn't sure why, though it undoubtedly had something to do with the case. Jamie had blasted her for agreeing to move out of Kate's. What could they do? Alex had argued back. They had no proof, no evidence, no suspects...nothing. Just a bunch of unconnected thoughts that were nagging at her, snapping, just on the verge of being an answer.

She picked up her cell phone to call Kate. "Come on," she whispered when Kate didn't pick up on the first ring. She didn't breathe again until the witness picked up, after the third ring.

"Hello?"

Alex breathed deeply, once.

"What is this?" Kate asked, and Alex could hear the teasing in her voice. "A heavy breather at the police department?"

"Just checking in," Alex answered.

"Well, all is well. I am going through my disco collection."

"I thought you hated disco."

"I do. I was young, naïve, and thought I looked good in platform shoes." There was a pause as Kate was interrupted by a knock on her door. "Really, Alex, a patrol is more than enough. I told you I don't want any cops in my house." Her tone was mildly exasperated.

"What? I didn't..."

"Then why is your good friend Andrew at my door?" There was a muffled conversation. "Okay, I will let him in for a split second so he can check all my doors, and then he's out of here. Goodnight, Detective Ryan."

The uneasiness intensified. *Andrew?* "Kate, wait; I don't ..." She stared at the dial tone. Kate had hung up. *It could be nothing. Maybe Andrew was on call tonight.* She pounded against her steering wheel as she redialed Kate's. After letting it ring and not getting an answer, she swore as she punched in numbers, holding back a scream of frustration. "He's got her."

"What?"

"Andrew."

"What? Alex, you're not making any sense."

"It's not making any sense to me, either. Meet me at Kate's. Hurry." She dialed Dispatch. "Where the hell is the watch? I personally asked to have them posted in front of 232 Springdale!" she yelled into the phone.

The dispatcher's voice came back eerily calm. "Detective Ryan, that order was rescinded."

"By who?"

"Officer Andrew Rhodes."

She flung the phone onto the seat. She knew with absolute certainty that she would see at least one death tonight. She just hoped she wouldn't be too late to also save one life.

KATE WATCHED WITH horror as Andrew ripped the phone cord from the wall.

"I was hoping that this would be over. I'm sorry, Kate. All I wanted was the diary."

"It was you standing at the elevator, wasn't it?" she asked softly.

He nodded. "She got greedy. What was I supposed to do? Christie had been blackmailing me for months with that damn diary. I tried to romance her, but it didn't work. All she wanted was more." He looked around, restless, then grabbed her. "Let's go. We don't have time for this." He pulled her to the door.

She saw his gun and knew that fighting would be futile. She remembered only too well what he had done to the last woman who had crossed him.

He laughed at the look on her face. "Don't worry. If I know Alex as well as I think, she'll know where to find us. She doesn't know it, but I've been reading her emails for weeks." He dropped a note on the table and pushed her outside.

ALEX ALMOST DROVE into the porch, braking at the last instant. She drew her gun and ran into Kate's house, but even before she began her search, she knew she was too late. A sudden noise made her flatten herself against the wall, and when the door creaked closed, she jumped out with her gun drawn.

Jamie collapsed against the wall. "Jesus!"

"Sorry." She released a breath. "He's got her."

"Who? Andrew?"

"Yeah."

Jamie shook her head. "It doesn't make any sense. What the hell is going on?"

"I wish I knew." Alex rubbed her forehead, then her eyes caught the note on the table. There was only one phrase scribbled on it, but it made Alex blanch. She threw it down and ran out.

Jamie called after her, "Alex, wait up!" but heard the tires screech as Alex roared away. She bent down and picked up the note. *Sorry about Sam.* A look of horror crossed her face. "Oh my God."

BACK IN THE alley for the first time since that long-ago night, Alex inched her way along the wall, gun drawn. As before, part of her registered the sounds around her. From force of habit, she searched the darkness for any signs of life. It was like revisiting a nightmare, with no hope of a different ending.

"I knew you'd figure it out." Andrew stepped from the shadows, one arm holding a terrified Kate, his gun against her temple. "Now what?"

Alex lifted her gun and aimed it straight at his heart. "Drop the gun, Andrew. Whatever this is, it's over."

"Really? Not from where I sit." He smiled. "Do you really want another one on your conscience, Alex?"

Alex flinched. "Why, Andy?"

He shrugged, looking pale. "I didn't know what to do, Alex. I got hooked on coke and I started to owe a bunch of money. Sam ended up helping me." He seemed lost in thought. "I didn't mean to hurt her. It was a mistake."

At his words, Alex felt the pain tighten in her chest but forced herself to inch forward, her eyes fixed on his gun. "How did Sam help you?" she asked softly, trying to distract him by keeping him talking.

He pulled Kate closer. "She gave me some stuff to tide me over."

"What stuff?"

He started to laugh. "Jesus, you didn't know?" He shook his head. "Whenever there was a bust of some sort, she skimmed a little off the top. Sold it. Who would bitch about a few grams missing here and there? Even if they did, who would believe a pusher's complaint?"

Alex watched him in horror. He didn't notice.

"Man, she was something. She even got that Billings guy to go rough up some of her collars when they started to make too much noise. Every time he got in trouble, she would show up and take over, became his private officer. Then I started to think—why shouldn't I get a bigger part of things?"

He saw the look on her face and it made him angry. "Why the fuck not? But she got pissed about it and threatened to sell me out. I couldn't have that. I just wanted to scare her; I didn't want to hurt her. I thought I could get Billings to help me reason with her."

Alex looked at him as if seeing him for the first time. The words buzzed inside her head and she felt a metallic taste in her mouth like bile. She swallowed hard, trying to keep herself from throwing up. Her chest constricted and she fought for breath, willing her hands to stop shaking.

"I guess I panicked when I saw you. It was an accident. I didn't mean to kill her," he whined. "I thought you had seen me." He looked like he was about to cry.

"You bastard." Alex fought for calm as she felt the rage almost blind her. Her finger tightened on the trigger, the hate flowing so intensely through her that it scared her. Her eyes tried not to glance at Kate. She needed to concentrate on him. If she didn't, Kate would be her undoing. "Let her go, Andrew. She has nothing to do with this. Don't make it any worse."

He laughed. "On the contrary..." He released the safety. "So, who wants to go first?"

Alex didn't waver. "Let her go. Don't make me do this."

"Do what? Shoot me?" He laughed. "What if you miss and hit her instead? Your hands shaking yet?"

The betrayal of all she had thought she knew threatened to bring her to her knees. Alex felt the nightmare tighten its grip around her, pulling her back to the wreckage of her memories of the night Sam died. She fought against the rising panic, tasted the saltiness of tears on her lips, shook her head, trying to clear it. Unbidden, the image of Megan floated to the surface; with it came clarity. Her voice broke as she said sadly, "We're supposed to be the good guys, Andy."

He sighed, looking defeated for a moment. "Good guys finish last. Sorry, Alex." The sound of the gun echoed long after the shot was fired.

Chapter
Twenty-Three

ARRIVING AT THE alley in time to see the final confrontation, Jamie had watched in terror at the fateful moment when Alex pulled the trigger and killed someone she had thought of as a brother. Then, with a mixture of relief and resentment, had watched Kate run to Alex. And now she watched her friend grieve—almost to the edge of madness. Alex grieved for an ideal destroyed, and for a woman she had never known—though she had thought she did. And Jamie waited it out.

Like a wounded animal, Alex retreated into herself and hid for days. Only Jamie was allowed near; and even that was a battle that threatened, at times, to turn physical. Afraid for her friend, she did not back down, could not back down despite Alex's anger at not being left alone. Apprehensive, she hid Alex's gun from her, fearing that Alex would, in a moment of weakness, go searching for it.

On more than one occasion, she had to physically restrain Madison and Darcy from barging in. She knew that when Alex was ready, she would let them know. The girls didn't like it but waited it out as well, helpless to ease their friend's hurt.

Finally, after three weeks, Alex came down, dressed, and asked for coffee. Jamie hid her relief and silently passed her a cup. Alex sat on a stool by the breakfast bar and took a sip. "Jamie, I wanted to...I just..." Alex looked away.

"I know. And you're welcome." They looked at each other, unable to find the words to express more. Too much had happened. Yet, here they were.

"Did you know any of this?" Alex finally asked.

Jamie sighed. "Some. I was starting to look into it the night Sam died. We had been getting accusations from defense lawyers who were charging that some of the money and even some of the drugs were missing. At first—you hear it, you ignore it. But when it's different lawyers at different times and they are reporting the same thing, someone eventually pays attention. Internal Affairs was starting to look into it, but then Sam died and that suspicion died with her. I don't think anyone had the stomach to continue searching with an election just around the corner. I think they were all afraid of the answers, so they canned the investigation. I didn't want you to think badly of her, so I didn't say anything. What was the point? The grief alone was enough for you to deal with. Andrew, though, was a surprise," Jamie admitted, her eyes flashing, feeling the white heat of rage flood through her. She released a slow breath, trying to stay calm.

"I feel foolish that I never suspected either of them. I never saw anything. How could I not see?" Alex asked. "I mean, I was living with her."

Jamie's touch on her face was gentle. "Alex, sometimes we are just too close to a situation. It happens. She covered her tracks well. She fooled us all." The shock of that still rankled.

They sat in silence as they finished their coffee. Finally, Jamie captured Alex's gaze. "Megan called to see how you were."

"Did she? Why?" Her tone was disinterested, but it did not fool Jamie.

Jamie rolled her eyes. "Maybe because she's worried about you. She heard about what happened."

Alex ignored the comment. She looked up from her cup and noted her friend's tired face. "You are a sight."

"Shut up." Jamie poured more coffee and took a sip. If she stopped moving, the headache would go away. Or at least she hoped so.

"Where did you go last night? Get lucky?" Alex asked. She had gone to bed after three and had been surprised to see that Jamie was not yet home.

"I just got in, actually." Jamie leaned against the counter, the coffee cupped between her palms.

Alex looked at her, a smirk slowly appearing on her face. "Wow, lucky you. Who's the woman? Anyone I know?"

"Yeah." Jamie looked back at her steadily. "I was with Megan."

For a moment the air seem to vibrate. "Funny, for a moment there I thought you said Megan."

Jamie blew gently on the steaming cup. She liked Megan and couldn't stand seeing her so broken up, especially since she knew that Alex was equally miserable. Last night after Megan had called, she had finally gone to check things out for herself. She had not been at all surprised to see a woman still in love, albeit confused and hurt. That this one was too stupid to figure it out pissed her off. She hated foolish people. She knew she was playing dangerously close to the line, but it would be worth it if it woke Alex up to the real possibility of forever losing someone she loved. "I *was* with

Megan."

If Jamie knew anything about anything, it was that Megan was perfect for Alex. She tried to pretend that she was not playing matchmaker; that went seriously against her image. And if confronted by any of them she would vigorously deny it. She braced herself. It didn't take long.

Alex jumped up, the chair crashing to the floor behind her. "Are you fucking kidding me? You and Megan?"

"She's single, so am I. You're done with her. Hell, this wouldn't be the first time I've dated one of your exes." In a perverse way, Jamie was actually enjoying pushing the buttons, almost laughing at the look on Alex's face.

Alex's eyes were hot, and her hands clenched into fists for a brief moment as she wanted to hit Jamie. She fought the panic that was making breathing hard. *Jamie and Megan. There is no way I could live with that.* "Back off, Jamie."

Jamie immediately relented. There was only so much toying she wanted to do. She cared for Alex too much to let her go on believing that anything was going on. She put her cup on the counter, then grabbed a strand of dark hair and tugged with just enough pressure. "Alexandra, I never took you for a coward." She brought her face close and stared at her. "You should go see her. It's not too late, believe me. I talked to her last night."

"No."

"Are you going to stand there and tell me that you are not still in love with her?"

"Dammit! And what if I am? She made it obvious it was over. She told me to leave." She didn't mention Megan asking her to stay the last time she'd seen her. Thinking of that night, and the loss it made her feel so acutely, brought too much pain.

Jamie shook her head. "Gee. You are an idiot. Isn't she worth fighting for?"

"I don't see that it's any of your business." Alex's tone was icy.

"Wrong." Jamie kissed her on the mouth. "I love you more than life itself, and you're miserable. That makes it my business. Don't make me call the cavalry again. God knows they are feeling left out."

The damn woman always knows how to break through my defenses, Alex thought grumpily. "I wouldn't know where to start."

"Start by telling her the truth. Tell her you love her."

Alex was frustrated. "I tried. The night we broke up."

Jamie looked at her with a mixture of amusement and pity. "Honey, that is the wrong time. No one listens when they're hurt. Their reaction is usually to try to shut off access, so as not to get hurt any worse."

"I don't know, Jamie. She made it pretty clear where she stood. I hurt her; but worse, I think—I disappointed her."

"I know you did. But someone has to swallow her pride and beg for forgiveness. My money is on you."

Alex looked at her, then away. She frowned. "I'm not very good at this relationship thing."

"Who is? Do you think any of us are? We try, that's all anyone can do. There are no instruction manuals, regardless of what the so-called relationship gurus say. This isn't like in the movies where everything becomes neat and tidy by the end of the final act. Being with someone takes a lot of work, constant work. And there are no guarantees that the relationship will last, even if you do all you can. With Sam, you did the best you could with what you had at the time. None of this was your fault. Don't let what happened with Sam stop you from taking a chance on something that could really make you happy. No two relationships are ever alike because *we* are never the same. Different people bring different things out in us.

"You've always had too much pride, Alex. That's your biggest fault. But if you love her...well, there is no pride when it comes to love." Something crossed Jamie's face, the flash of a memory where pride had stopped her from taking a chance; then her face cleared. "What's the worst that can happen? She's already dumped you." She had to laugh at the glare on Alex's face.

"You know, there are days when I really don't like you. You just did this so it would piss me off, didn't you?" Jamie laughed as she left the room. "Jamie?" Alex called out after her.

"Yeah?"

"You should take your own advice and go see Kate."

"Shut up. And who says I haven't? Anyway, I refuse to be anyone's experiment, and that is all it would be. She's only toying with the idea."

AS AN ACT of closure, Alex went to the cemetery and stood staring at the white marble tombstone. She stood for a long moment under the bright sunshine and thought about everything that had happened: the shock of finding out it had been Sam all along; the moment she'd pulled the trigger. She felt no satisfaction from having followed her instincts to such a devastating conclusion, though part of her wished she hadn't. Sometimes ignorance was bliss.

It was her first visit in months, and she stood under the noon sun and tried to remember the woman she had once loved so completely. *Ten years of being with someone who turns out to be a stranger.* That was the most painful discovery, the hardest thing to accept. *To live with someone, love someone, and not know them at all... Is love so blind that you don't see what you don't want to see?* She really couldn't answer that.

Regardless, she had avenged Sam's death twice. In her twelve years as an officer, she had pulled the trigger twice, and both times it had been because of Sam. Now she was there to say a final good-bye. Goodbye to a woman she had loved, but not enough... and to a man she had called a friend; to her memory of them in her life; to a life she had thought she understood. But Jamie was right—none of it was her fault. She had done the best she could with what she knew. That was all anyone could ever hope for. She felt the weight lift from her shoulders. It was time to move on. *Or at least, time to start trying.* She had another stop to make.

When she turned, her eyes caught a camel-colored coat and she recognized Stacey standing several feet away. Hesitating, they stared at each other for a moment. With a faint smile, Alex walked toward her.

"We never really knew her, did we?" Stacey asked quietly.

Alex looked back at the gravesite. "We knew what she wanted us to know, I guess."

Stacey nodded and turned to go, the pain evident on her face, her eyes troubled.

"Hey, Stacey?" She turned and looked at Alex standing by the dirt road. "Why don't you come over for dinner one night next week?"

Stacey nodded once and turned to go. She never looked back.

Chapter
Twenty-Four

THE PARCEL ARRIVED the following week. Megan puzzled over the box sitting on the floor. She lifted her eyes to Willy, who had dropped by for tea. "It's made out to me, but there's no return address."

Willy clapped her hands together in delight. "Ooh...I do love surprises. Open it."

Megan opened the box and pushed the crumpled paper aside. Her eyes filled with tears at what she found. "Winnie the Pooh." She started to cry.

Willy fussed over her worriedly. "Oh, honey, what's wrong. Did you hurt yourself?"

"They're from Alex." Megan held a book pressed against her chest. She pulled out the books, one by one. Somehow, the entire collection of *Winnie the Pooh* was inside. "And they're first editions, too." A fresh batch of tears followed.

"I see." Willy hid a smile. "Well, isn't that sweet of her?"

"Yes. No, it's not sweet. It's..." She brushed the tears away. "Damn her. What am I going to do?" She held the book pensively.

Willy looked up and saw Alex hesitating at the door. "Well, here's your chance to find out." She hustled away as Megan looked up.

Alex's eyes drank her in. "Hi."

"Hi." Megan looked down at the books then up again. "I don't know what to say."

"Say thanks," she suggested

"Thank you; but, Alex, I..."

"Listen, Megan, can we talk?"

Megan, feeling weakened, shook her head. "I don't think that's a good idea."

Alex felt the fist slam in her gut, but she didn't back down. "Probably not, but just the same..." She drew in a deep breath. "I just want five minutes."

Megan turned to look for Willy, who had discreetly tiptoed out. "How are you?" she finally asked.

Alex pushed her hands into the front pockets of her jeans. "Okay." She frowned.

"Are you back at work?"

"Next week. They usually give you leave after a shooting. They make you go to a psychologist and stuff." She shifted, not wanting to get distracted from what she had come to say.

"Can I see your badge?"

"What? I don't..." When Megan continued to look back at her calmly, she shook her head, frustrated. "Sure." She pulled out her gold shield and handed it over.

Megan took it, studied it, opened and closed the wallet a few times. "How does it feel?"

"Right." She slipped it back in her pocket. "You were right all along. I shouldn't have left the force."

"You just needed some time to grieve." Megan looked at her for a beat. *It's time to clear the air.* "Alex, I know that we were in a difficult position before. I might have been unkind. I'm sorry for that. I'm also sorry about Sam. When I heard what just happened, well...I tried to reach you." She didn't add that she had been hurt that Alex had refused to take her call, feeling foolish that she had misread the tentative steps they had taken by spending the evening together.

"I know. You were right; everything you said was right. I didn't want you to get too close, and I made certain you couldn't. You were one of the main reasons I was able to go back to work, but sharing it with you would have meant it mattered, that what you thought of me mattered. I was scared." She turned, rolling her shoulders to release the tension.

Megan looked at her quietly. "There's no point in raking it up again. It's done. I have to take some responsibility, too. I behaved arrogantly. You hurt me, but I didn't give you a chance to explain." She shifted against the weight of her admission. "Truthfully, I didn't want to hear your side. It might have shown that I wasn't completely blameless. I wasn't exactly forthcoming in how I felt either. I'm sorry for that."

Alex's hands clenched by her side. Begging was so alien to her. "Megan, I've been miserable. I miss you like crazy." Megan's eyes flickered but she said nothing. Alex rushed on before she lost her nerve. "I don't sleep. I don't eat. Jamie's just about ready to either kick me out or beat my brains in. I'm sure she told you. She even called me an idiot." Megan had to smile at that. Filled with nervous energy, Alex started to pace. "I came here today to beg you for another chance." *There, I said it.* She stopped with her back to

Megan, unable to bear seeing the rejection on her face. She braced herself for its verbal counterpart.

Megan looked at the books on the floor, then back at Alex. "I'm not sure what another chance might entail," she said cautiously.

Alex turned and her eyes were filled with raw feelings. "Whatever this is between us scares the hell out of me, but I can't turn away from it. Somehow, while I wasn't paying attention, you reached in and dug yourself a place in my heart; and I can't fill it unless you're with me. I've been walking wounded for a long time, yet caring about you is healing me." She shook her head, spreading her hands wide. "I guess my heart knew all along; it just took some time for my mind to catch up. I love you, Megan. I would like an opportunity to show you this time. To start over and show you that you are all the way in. I won't keep anything from you ever again."

That stopped Megan cold. She sighed, resigned to the fact that there wasn't any doubt as to what would happen next. "Damn you." But her tone was gentle, the look in her eyes even more so.

It sent shivers up Alex's spine and she smiled slowly, hope rising. "Yeah."

"These books were a direct hit. You really don't play fair."

"I was desperate." She took a step forward. Waited.

"Well, hell." Megan shook her head and smiled slowly. "I guess I love you, too. We are a pair."

"Yeah. That's what Jamie says." Alex closed the distance between them and touched Megan's mouth with a gentle hand.

Megan felt the tingle of it to her bones. "If we do this, you'd better not shut me out...ever."

"I promise."

"We talk about everything."

"Everything."

"And we're keeping the phone."

Alex made a show of thinking about it, then she shrugged. "Okay."

"And I swear, if I have any more problems with you, I'm becoming celibate."

"God forbid!" Alex's mouth closed on Megan's, the blood roaring in her ears. Her tongue slipped into the welcoming wet warmth to toy and tease. Megan's mouth heated under her incursion. They pulled apart slowly and stared at each other in wonder. "I'm crazy about you. Thanks for waiting for me," Alex whispered.

"Ditto, and you're welcome."

Epilogue

AT FIRST THE form bundled under the white sheet never moved, but the irritating noise persisted and slowly, with a groan, Alex buried her head under the pillow. Beside her, a muffled voice cursed. "Ignore them, they will go away."

The banging continued, interspersed with the ringing of the buzzer. "They're like gnats—they never go away."

Alex lifted her head and peered at the clock beside the bed. She blinked once, twice, trying to believe that it was not 7 a.m. But the green numbers seem to glow sarcastically back at her: 'Yep, it's 7 a.m.' She sat up, the sheet falling down to her bare waist, and pushed a hand through her tangled hair. Frustrated, she wanted to scream but didn't dare. *How much wine did we drink last night?*

Beside her, Megan burrowed further under the duvet. Alex's hand caressed the smooth back under the covers, and for a moment she considered lying back down and letting her hands wander. The shrill ringing of the doorbell interrupted her thoughts. With a curse, she swung her long legs out of bed and rested her feet on the bare floor. She tested the strength in her legs before rising. *Not bad. Walking shouldn't be too difficult. Just one step after the other.* She fished around the tangled sheets for her robe and pulled it on.

"Honey, what is it?" a voice from deep under the covers called out.

"Nothing for you to worry about. Go back to sleep." With a last lingering look at Megan's recumbent form, she stalked into the living room where the pounding continued. With a snarl she opened the door, and glared at the two women with one eye, the other remaining firmly shut against the morning brightness.

"You guys have got to find yourselves girlfriends, or pets...something."

Unfazed, Jamie and Darcy stood in the hallway grinning as they sipped their coffee. Then Jamie straightened from where she leaned casually on the doorframe, and offered Alex a cup.

"So, what the hell do you want?" Alex asked.

"We have to do something about Madison."

Alex accepted the cup and looked back with longing at the bedroom, fighting the tempting memory of the warm covers and the smooth naked body awaiting her. Saying a silent goodbye, she sighed as she swung the door wider to let them in. *So much for sleeping in.* She turned to them. "What's wrong with Madison?"

"She's making a mess of things since her break-up with Lauren."

"No doubt."

"She's not eating; she's not sleeping; she's talking about quitting her practice. What we need is an intervention," Jamie continued.

Alex sighed as she took a sip of coffee. *Life sure isn't boring.* As she looked at their determined faces, she felt the love wash through her and knew that this was always going to be the way of it. *We have lived our lives in each other's presence*, she thought. *How could it be otherwise?* "Okay, then. Let's go intervene."

The End.

Also available from
Jessica Casavant
and
Yellow Rose Books

Twist of Fate

Journalist Lauren Taylor is sleepwalking through her life and knows it. When her husband, US senator Matt Taylor, announces that he is running for the US Presidency, Lauren knows that she will need to make a decision about her life. Shortly after Matt's bombshell, Lauren attends a funeral where she meets Madison Williams, a doctor who has learned to disengage from life. Intrigued and feeling an immediate connection, the two women start to spend time together, until one weekend when their growing attraction is acted upon. Their affair continues until a devastating discovery and its aftermath, forces Lauren to make a choice. She bows to the inevitability of her life and stays with her husband.

Two years later, Lauren sees her past resurface when Keith McGraw, an ambitious journalist confronts her with proof of her affair with Madison. The threat of exposure starts a chain of events that forces Lauren to re-examine her life's choices and the future path she will take. Does she deny everything, and become what she does not want to be – First Lady? Or does she confront what she has been running away from for years?

Sometimes it takes a twist of fate to shake you out of a self-induced coma or so Lauren Taylor comes to believe.

ISBN 1-932300-07-4

Jessica Casavant is an award-winning recording engineer, who decided the night a fist fight broke out between two actors that she had had enough. There is only so much of someone else's vision a woman should take. She now works in the television industry while spinning stories on the side. *Twist of Fate* was her first published novel that started the Boston friends' series. She is at work on her 3rd novel *Imperfect Past* which will be Jamie's story. She can be reached at cdjc@sympatico.ca and www.jessicacasavant.com.

Printed in the United States
21800LVS00005B/14

9 781932 300208